BAD INTENTIONS

INTENTIONS DUET #1

ELLA FRANK

Copyright © 2021 by Ella Frank
www.ellafrank.com
Edited by Arran McNicol
Cover Design: By Hang Le
Cover Photography by Miguel Anxo
Cover Model: Sergio Carvajal

No part of this book may be reproduced in any form or by any electronic or mechanical means, including information storage and retrieval systems, without written permission from the author, except for the use of brief quotations in a book review.

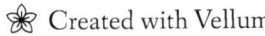 Created with Vellum

CHAPTER 1

GABE

I HATE INTERVIEWS. I'd rather go to the dentist than to one of these things. But as I sat in one of the most impressive offices I'd ever set foot inside of, I knew that this particular interview could either make me or break me.

This job right here was the key to my future. It was the stepping stone to getting back on the real course my life was meant to be on, instead of this little detour it had taken over the last six months.

To do that, however, I had to survive the cut. I wasn't the first to step inside this office this morning. I'd been waiting out in the lobby for the past two hours and seen many come and go. But as I finally took my place front and center, opposite a desk that looked more expensive than everything I owned, I knew this was it.

I needed to project confidence, be eager—but not overeager—and manage to land the opportunity of a lifetime. Sure, no problem. I could do that.

"Mr. Romero, so sorry to keep you waiting."

At the sound of the office door opening behind me, I turned to see the man I was here to interview with today step inside. I'd done my due diligence in researching Mitchell & Madison Attorneys at Law, but the impact of Logan Mitchell in person caught me completely off guard.

In a grey suit with hair black as coal, the man was striking in a way that left you almost dumbfounded, as he crossed the room and made his way around the desk to his chair.

I smoothed my hand down my tie, the confidence from my little pep talk seconds ago quickly vanishing, as I tried to remember all of the reasons why *I* was the best fit for this job.

Mr. Mitchell took a seat and reached for the black-framed glasses on his desk, then he picked up my resumé and scanned the document. I was glad for the reprieve, because I needed the extra seconds to pull myself together and remember how to, oh, I don't know, speak.

"Okay, Mr. Romero. Gabriel, is it?"

"Yes. Gabriel, but I usually go by Gabe."

"Okay, Gabe." Mr. Mitchell gave me a tight smile that did nothing to help ease my nerves. "I'm Logan Mitchell, one of the owners and partners here at Mitchell & Madison, and as you know, I'm looking for a new personal assistant."

I rested my hands on my thighs and resisted the urge to wipe them dry, as I tried to remember everything I'd read and learned about this place.

"Your resumé looks good, if a little sparse on the experience side of things. But I'm more interested in what you have to tell me about yourself than what's on a piece of paper. So for the moment, let's do that, and see how we go."

Okay, well, that was kind of refreshing. I'd expected to have to go on the defense about my lack of job experience, since I'd been busy doing other things over the past three years. But talk about myself? I could do that. I knew I could do this job and do it well, and now I just had to convince him.

"First off, I'd like to thank you for the opportunity to be here today. It's a privilege to even be considered for a job at a firm as reputable as this one. As you can see on my resumé there, I've been a full-time student for the past three years at Northwestern University."

"I did see that." Mr. Mitchell leaned back in his seat and steepled his fingers over his chest. "I went there myself, as did my brother, who is also one of the owners and partners here."

I knew that. I'd done my research. Logan Mitchell and Cole Madison had both graduated from Pritzker School of Law. It was ranked one of the top fourteen law schools in the U.S. So it was no surprise that they had gone on to build one of the most successful law firms in the country. A place anybody would be proud to work at, myself included.

"I read that. It's one of the other reasons I was so excited to receive a callback. I like the idea of working for a fellow Northwesterner."

Mr. Mitchell's lips twitched as he eyed me from behind

his glasses. "You said the past three years? You're no longer in school?"

"I'm not, no." I'd known this question would come up, and even though it was a difficult one, I'd crafted an answer I hoped would satisfy. "Due to unexpected circumstances, I had to withdraw from my course early. But I hope to one day to be able to go back, maybe at night, and finish my degree."

Mr. Mitchell's eyes narrowed, but he didn't push for any more than that. "I hope so too. Let's get started, then, shall we? Why don't you tell me why you want to work here? Beyond the two of us being fellow Northwesterners, that is."

I aimed my most winning smile his way and did my very best to project confidence as I ran over my spiel in my head. There were a few reasons I wanted to work for this company, and this man in particular. Some of which were professional, and one very important fact that was extremely personal—not that I was about to bring up his marriage and personal life. That was just a bonus, something I came across when I was researching him.

Right now, it was time to sell him on me. To let him know that I'd put an effort into today, spent time learning about the company I wanted to be hired at, and give him no reason to question the fact that *I* was the perfect fit for this job.

"As I've thought about my next move, career-wise, it's important to me to work for a company with strong values. Values that are similar to my own. I know you went up against the big pharma companies in a lawsuit against

Berivax. You did a lot of good for a lot of people, and not many are willing to stand up against the big companies for fear of losing. You did it anyway."

Mr. Mitchell said nothing in the face of my praise, and that was understandable. He knew how badass he was for winning that case. Hell, it had made his company shoot to the number one spot among law firms in the country. But still, it was worth mentioning, in my opinion, as was what I said next.

"I'd also like to work for a company that has a positive work environment, and I can't think of anything more positive than what you did for those families."

"Agreed. That was a very good day and years in the making. It took a lot of hard work, long hours, and dedication from many people here at the firm. My personal assistant included."

In other words: *You get this job, you'll be expected to work when I need you to work, no questions asked.*

Message received.

Mr. Mitchell sat forward, his eyes cutting to the resumé in front of him. "It says here you were the event coordinator for Queertopia in 2020 at Northwestern."

I was wondering if he'd bring that up. I'd hoped he would, because it not only showed another commonality between us, but also my kickass organizational skills.

"Yes. I was involved in 2019 and again in 2020. I'm an extremely organized person and naturally obsessive about timetables and schedules."

"Maybe I should get you to talk to my husband. He's always late."

"Oh, okay. I'm always on time. Usually early, if I'm being honest."

"That's not a bad habit to have. Please, continue."

Right, what was I talking about again? Oh, that's right, myself.

"I enjoy working with a diverse group of people who each bring something new to the table and listen and respect one another. I get along with practically everyone, and I'm an extremely hard worker. I will always try my very best to do or get whatever it is you need, and if there's something I can't do, then I'll find someone who can help me. I believe I would be a great fit for you, and I would enjoy the opportunity to prove that."

He nodded and looked at me over the top of his glasses. "And what about weakness? What would you say is one of yours?"

I hated this question. Why would I want to tell him what I'm not good at? It was a trick, one disguised to trip you up and leave you tongue-tied. But I'd come with a game plan that would hopefully win him over, because I *really* wanted this job.

"I guess one of my biggest weaknesses is that I've always had a lot of curiosity and energy, and sometimes that leads me into taking on too much at one time."

Mr. Mitchell picked up the pen on his desk and wrote something across the top of my resumé. Then he sat back in his chair and looked me over with quiet contemplation.

Be cool, Gabe. Keep it together. You haven't messed up once. Don't start now.

"I like you, Mr. Romero—Gabe." He tapped the arm of his chair. "This job won't be easy."

"I don't want easy." In fact, I was hoping it would keep me so busy I could forget the reason I needed it in the first place. "I want to work somewhere that I can be proud of and that I can enjoy day in and day out."

Mr. Mitchell sat forward and handed me my resumé. "Take this out to Tiffany at the front desk. She's going to tell you where to go to get your drug test. Once that's cleared, she'll give you a call so you can come in and get everything set up with HR."

My jaw practically hit the floor as what he was telling me began to register.

Holy shit. Did I just... Did I just get the job?

"Gabe? Was there something else you wanted to ask?"

I took the piece of paper from him and shook my head. "No. I'm sorry." I couldn't help the smile that stretched across my face. "I just... I wasn't expecting an answer right now, and I'm very happy."

"Ah, okay. Yes, well, Sherry won't be happy that I didn't go through the rest of the bunch sitting out there, but like I said, I like you. I've sat through more interviews this morning than I care to ever again, and you're the first person I didn't want to strangle."

My eyes widened as a devilish grin crossed his lips, and I had a feeling that *this* version of Logan Mitchell was the true version. Not the cool-as-a-cucumber professional who had just grilled me.

He chuckled. "I think you're going to fit in here very well, Gabe. As long you don't go home and get high as a kite tonight."

I almost choked. "Of course not, Mr. Mitchell."

"Logan."

"Excuse me?"

"Mr. Mitchell makes me feel...old, and I hate that. If you're going to work for me day in and day out, you can call me Logan."

"Yes, Mr.—Logan."

"Good. Well then." *Logan* got to his feet and held out his hand for me to shake, and it took everything I had not to jump up and fist-bump the air. "I look forward to seeing you next week. Have a good weekend."

Uh, I was going to have the best weekend ever now. His decision to hire me had literally just changed my life, and that, in my opinion, was cause to celebrate.

CHAPTER 2

MARCUS

"YOU MUST BE pleased with yourself after seeing today's numbers."

I stared across my desk to where my boss and owner of Tennant Broadcasting, Gloria Tennant, was sitting with a smug look on her face, and couldn't disagree with that assessment. The ratings for this quarter were well above average, America having decided to once again place their trust in our hands as ENN reclaimed its place at the top of all broadcasting news companies.

That was good for me as the president of ENN Worldwide news division, but for Gloria? It was music to her ears. I'd just made her a hell of a lot richer this morning, as stocks for the company soared.

"I'm definitely not disappointed. The last four months have been difficult, to say the least. We've had to put up with a lot. It's nice to see some acknowledgment of that."

"I agree, and while much of that has to do with the faces

and reliability of the news your colleagues deliver day in and day out, I'm well aware of who is steering this ship, Marcus."

That was good to know, and Gloria's subtle way of reminding me of my upcoming contract renegotiation. Not that I needed reminding. I was well aware that this news would lead to a bidding war on my head, and so was Gloria, which was why she'd travelled down from her tower to meet with me this evening.

"Will you be attending tonight's celebration?" I already knew the answer to that would be no. But it was the easiest way to deviate from a conversation revolving around my future employment when I had no contract in front of me and—I looked to the empty tumbler on my desk—one glass of scotch already in me.

"No. I'm actually on my way out of town for the weekend. I trust you'll pass on my congratulations to the rest of the staff?"

"I will. You'll be missed."

Gloria chuckled and reached up to play with the bulbous pearls of her necklace. "Don't lie, Marcus—you're terrible at it. The staff will have a much more enjoyable time without me there to make them check themselves every five minutes."

While that was true, I wasn't about to say so. Gloria was a ball buster, and everyone on the ENN crew knew you watched your Ps and Qs around her. But if we were handing out invitations based on that particular quality, I should probably remove myself from the guest list also. I wasn't exactly known for my jovial nature.

"Before I go, I also wanted to fill you in on the new change we're making with our law firm."

"Oh?" That was news. ENN had been working with the same law firm for as long as I'd been here. From contracts, to lawsuits, to general advice, we'd always used Hoffman & Associates.

"Yes. Jeremiah suddenly wants to up our retainer fee, and I'm suspecting it has to do with our success this past year."

Bad move, Jeremiah. The one thing Gloria expected above all else when it came to her company was loyalty. Greed would not go over well.

"If he thinks I'm just going to roll over and take that kind of treatment, he has another thing coming. If anything, he should be rewarding our years of loyalty, not demanding more money. Weasel. How many clients has he retained through me?"

Hundreds, I was sure.

"Anyway, I'd appreciate you setting up a meeting with this new firm I'm interested in. They've recently been named the top firm in the country, and they're right here in Chicago. Let's see what their pricing runs at. If I can have the best for the same price Jeremiah is coming at me with, I'm not going to settle."

"I'll have Carmen set it up tonight."

"Not tonight, Marcus." Gloria got to her feet. "She can do it next week. Tonight, go and enjoy yourself and congratulate your staff. That's an order."

I raised an eyebrow.

"I know you hate those, but yes. Tonight, that's what I'm giving you, an order. You've worked nonstop this year. You deserve a night off to enjoy yourself. You do remember how to do that, don't you?"

I stood up and buttoned my suit jacket. "Happy?"

"Thrilled."

"Alexander's on in ten. Things will get underway after that. Are you sure you don't want to stay?"

"Harold is waiting downstairs. If I take any longer, he'll leave me."

"He wouldn't dare."

Gloria smirked as we walked to my door and I pulled it open for her. She was just about to step through when she stopped and gave me an assessing look.

"And you—would you dare to leave me?"

There was a reason Gloria had remained the face of her father's company when he stepped down. She was cunning and calculating. She was also smart as a whip. But I'd been working for her long enough to know her moves, and I wasn't about to fall for this one.

Her eyes narrowed at my silence, but she gave a clipped nod. If there was one thing she appreciated more than loyalty, it was brains, and while she'd just tried to trip me up, I could tell she respected my desire to keep my cards close. After all, that was what she'd do.

"Very well, I'll leave you to it. Have a good night, Marcus. We'll catch up next week."

I inclined my head and watched after her as she made her way to her private elevator. Once she was gone, I shut my office door and made my way down the hall to where Carmen, my personal assistant, sat.

"If you need me, I'm going to be sitting in on Alexander's broadcast."

"Very good, sir."

I turned to make my way over to the main elevator banks, but at the last second stopped. "Carmen?"

"Yes, sir?"

"Why don't you shut it down for the night and get ready for the party?"

Her eyes widened, and I realized just how out of character it was for me to tell her to stop work under any circumstance. But if I was being ordered to go and have a good night, then she should too.

"Umm..."

To save her from trying to tell me she was okay with working until the end of her shift, I said, "I'll see you there."

Her brow furrowed as though she was trying to decide if I was messing with her, but then she nodded. Satisfied I'd gotten my point across, I entered the now-open elevator and hit the down button.

When I reached ENN's main floor, I was pleased to note I'd be just in time to catch *Global News*'s opening segment. I walked across the newsroom and noted a couple of people behind computers still monitoring and gathering information for the late-night broadcasts, while several others chatted amongst themselves. As soon as they looked up and realized who it was walking through their workspace, however, they quickly feigned interest in the papers in their hands.

I was under no delusions when it came to my reputation around here. "Cutthroat and tenacious, with a heart of stone" was one of the many descriptions I'd heard thrown around, and that was fine by me. I ran the largest news organization in the country, and if that meant I gained respect by running things with a cool head and by a strict code, then that was the way it would be.

There was no room for error in this job. We led with facts that were double-, triple-, hell, quadruple-checked at times, and if they were wrong or messed up in any way at all, it wasn't only their asses on the line but mine. There were very real consequences for being wrong in this industry, and for that reason alone, I made sure to run the tightest of ships.

I pushed through the doors of Control Room A and spotted my top executive producer—Angela Davis—standing behind the large soundboard with her headset on and her eyes glued to the monitor, watching the country's most trusted news anchor.

Alexander Thorne.

He wore a crisp purple shirt and black suit and tie, and his blue eyes and silver hair made a striking picture up there on the screen with the vibrant blue set behind him. He was busy getting his mic in place and looking at the notes on the desk in front of him, and as I made my way down to the front of the control room, I spotted his fiancé, Sean Bailey, seated off to the side with a headset on.

"Sean."

Sean glanced my way and gave a clipped nod. "Marcus."

With our usual greeting out of the way, we returned our attention to the man we were both there to watch for very different reasons. "You're here for the party, I assume?"

"No way. I came to see you. I've missed our little chats."

I cast a droll look his way, making him laugh, before returning my attention to the monitor. Detective Sean Bailey had been a permanent fixture here a little while back when he'd taken on Alexander's security detail. But with the threat no longer an issue, he'd gone back to his day job with the Chicago PD. Something I wasn't at all upset about.

"Aw, come on, Marcus. Didn't you miss me? Even a little."

"So little, I didn't even realize it." I clasped my hands behind my back and glanced at the red countdown. Twenty seconds.

"You gonna be there?"

I looked down at Sean. "At the party?"

"Yeah."

"Considering I'm throwing it, I think people might see it as poor form if I don't show. Don't you?"

"I didn't think you'd care one way or another what people think—"

"I don't." I turned back to the monitor and timer—ten seconds. "Gloria does, and she told me I had to go and enjoy myself."

Sean laughed. "Well, that's definitely going to make my

night more interesting. I don't think I've *ever* seen you enjoy yourself."

I didn't anticipate he would tonight either. My goal was to get in and out of this thing as soon as possible. Just because I'd been ordered to attend, it didn't mean I had to do it with a smile on my face.

After I sent a final glare in the mouthy detective's direction, the control room fell silent and all attention focused on the screens.

"Good evening and welcome to Global News this Friday evening. I'm Alexander Thorne, and I thank you all for being here with me tonight..."

CHAPTER 3
GABE

"WOULD YOU STOP messing with your tie?"

I glanced over at my roommate and best friend, Ryan Carrigan, and tugged at the strip of material that I swear got tighter with every passing second.

"I wouldn't be messing with it if you hadn't made me wear it. I look like an uptight librarian."

"Trust me, you couldn't pass for a librarian if you tried. Uptight or otherwise. Plus, I didn't make you wear it. You asked what kind of party we were going to, and I said think suits and ties. That didn't mean you had to wear one."

I could practically hear his eyes roll as he punched the button of the elevator and the doors slid shut. We'd just arrived downtown at the building where Ryan's job at *Global News* was located.

Tonight, the bigwigs had decided to throw some kind of party after finding out their company had annihilated their competition in the ratings, and since we were both out to celebrate, Ryan had suggested I come with him.

Now, this wasn't exactly *my* idea of a good time on a Friday night, but it was free, something I very much appreciated with the current state of my bank account. Things would definitely be tight until my first paycheck came through in a couple of weeks. But the fact that I knew one was coming was enough.

"What else was I going to wear? You're in a suit and tie."

"That's because I work here. People expect me to dress a certain way."

"You're an assistant—"

"To Alexander *Thorne*, and trust me, he expects his staff to be as put together as he is. Kind of like your new bigwig lawyer is going to expect of *you*."

I gave Ryan a quick once-over and frowned. He was right; Logan had definitely given off the whole suit-and-tie vibe. But that was next week. I could worry about that then. Tonight, however, was a different story, and since I didn't actually *own* a suit right now, I'd borrowed this one from Ryan, and this tie had to go.

So as the elevator made its never-ending ascent to ENN's floor, I stuffed it in my back pocket, then popped free several of the top buttons and let out a sigh.

Ryan chuckled. "You should've just gone with that to begin with. Or that penguin suit of yours."

"That's a little *too* formal, don't you think?"

"Yeah, probably."

"And you sure this isn't too casual?"

"Oh, please. You could wear a paper bag and look good. You don't need me to tell you that."

I guess I'd have to trust him, because our elevator had just reached its destination. A loud *ding* announced our arrival, and when the doors slid open, we were face to face with Ryan's boss. Not his actual boss, but a gigantic poster of his face with the words *Global News with Alexander Thorne* across the image.

Well, if you didn't know who the star of this building was before you entered it, you certainly did stepping off on this floor. As we walked out into the hall, I leaned into Ryan's side.

"How do you ever get any work done with such a sexy boss?"

"I remind myself that he's taken and, you know, my *boss*. That generally works."

Yeah, I supposed it would. Two seconds in Logan's company and I'd somehow managed to block out the fact he was incredible to look at and quickly put him in the "untouchable boss" box too.

Ryan looked at me out of the corner of his eye. "Plus, Xander's totally not my type."

True, we were complete opposites when it came to that. Where Ryan wanted someone big and brawny, I was more about polished, mature, and...sexy.

"But forget about Xander. He's engaged, remember?"

"Oh, that's right. To his cop bodyguard."

"Yeah, Sean. Mhmm, now he's more my type. And he's super protective too."

I didn't doubt it. I remembered reading all about that stalker craziness when it had finally come out, and Ryan had been beside himself when his boss announced the news that he was getting engaged to the man who had saved him. It wouldn't have surprised me in the slightest if Ryan had made up a story to get a bodyguard all of his own with the way he'd been all dreamy-eyed over Sean.

"Okay, let's go. The party's being held in the conference room." Ryan headed off down the hall, and as I followed behind him, I noted an empty reception desk and an office that seemed to take up one side of the entire floor. But before I could ask whom it belonged to, we stopped at a set of double doors on the opposite side of the hall.

The conference room, I presumed.

"Wow. This place is something else."

"It's one of the *two* executive floors in the building. This one has the president's office and the conference room, and the one above it is for the owner. Pretty fancy, huh?"

"Fancy is an understatement."

"Wait until you get a look at the view inside. I've only ever been up here once before, but holy sh—"

"Ryan!" A blond woman with a perky ponytail smiled wide as she pulled open the door and spotted us.

"Stephanie. Hey."

"Hey. I was wondering when you'd get here." She took a sip out of the champagne glass she held and looked between the two of us.

"I told you earlier I was running home to get changed and pick up my friend."

"Oh, that's right. I totally forgot." She turned her attention my way. "And you must be the friend."

"That'd be me." I held out my hand. "I'm Gabe."

She slipped her hand into mine, and her smile changed from "hello" to...interested. Lucky for me, though, Ryan decided to step in and cut that off at the pass.

"I still haven't gotten over the fact that the Almighty opened up the golden gates tonight."

I had no idea what Ryan was talking about as he hooked an arm through Stephanie's elbow. But when we stepped inside, I totally tuned him out anyway, because *damn*, he hadn't been lying. The inside of the conference room was absolutely jaw-dropping.

Just as I'd suspected, it took up one side of the entire floor of the building. The interior was awash in shades of greys and blues, with gorgeous pieces of artwork hanging on the wall, each individually lit.

The far end of the room had a massive TV screen and podium on a stage, and the opposite wall was all glass. And while the view of downtown Chicago was impressive at night, what caught and held my attention was the rectangular light fixtures overhead. They reminded me of hundreds of crystal stalactites all hanging at different heights, and it appeared they could be muted or set to bright with the flick of a switch. It was stunning, and I was mesmerized.

"Gabe?"

"Yeah?" I blinked but couldn't look away as Stephanie moved up beside me.

"It's impressive, isn't it?"

"I can't stop looking at it. It's like an icy fortress or something up here."

Ryan laughed. "That's fitting."

"What do you mean?"

"Oh, nothing. Why don't we go and find some food and maybe a drink?"

"Sounds good to me. Lead the way."

Ryan and Stephanie took off ahead of me, and as I followed them into the crowd of people, I spotted several faces that were familiar. It was a strange sensation seeing someone you watched on TV in person. It was almost as though you knew them even though you'd never met.

Stephanie excused herself to go and chat with another couple, and when we stopped at the bar, Ryan looked at me and winked.

"So, what'll it be?"

"A dirty martini?"

"You got it, and I'll have a whiskey sour," Ryan said to the man behind the bar. Then we turned to look out at his coworkers as we waited.

Ryan had been right: the crowd varied in their appearances tonight from work clothes, to suits, to some in fine-dining attire. There was a slew of fashion choices, and I was happy to see that I fell somewhere in the middle.

"I told you it wasn't black tie, didn't I?"

"You did, but can you blame me for doubting you? Look at this place. It's not exactly the kind of party a college student frequents."

"*Ex*-college student. You're a career man now, just like the rest of us. Better get used to it."

"I don't know if I'll *ever* get used to that. It's not exactly the way I saw my life going."

"I know, but you'll get back on track. This is going to get you there. In the meantime, let's celebrate."

"Sir?" the bartender said from behind us, and Ryan turned to get our drinks. As he did, the crowd dispersed and my gaze landed on a man who had just handed off an empty martini glass to a passing waiter.

Alone, he stood away from the crowd, over by the wall of windows with his hands clasped behind his back and his spine straight and tall. His navy suit stretched across his broad shoulders, and his blond hair shone under the twinkling lights like gold—and just as I had been seconds earlier, I found myself mesmerized.

So much so that I took a step forward to go to him.

"Here you go." Ryan handed me my drink.

Without taking my eyes off the man who'd captured my attention, I took the glass. "Who's that?"

The music and people in the room seemed to fade away as I willed the stranger by the windows to turn around.

"Who's wh— Oh no. No way. Whatever you're thinking, stop, right now."

Ryan stepped in front of me, blocking my view, and I all but cracked my neck in an effort to see around him.

"Hey? Focus." Ryan clicked his fingers in front of my face, then glanced over his shoulder to where the man still stood, silent and stunning in his solitude.

"Who is that?"

Ryan shook his head as he looked back at me. "*That* is out of your league, is what that is."

I pulled a face as Ryan sighed and stood next to me again.

"Look, I know you're used to going after whoever you want, and that the word no is more of a challenge to you than a deterrent. But that's Marcus St. James. This floor is *his* floor. He's the president of ENN Worldwide. He's big fish, and you, my friend, are an itty-bitty one."

Marcus St. James. Even his name was hot, and while I heard what Ryan was saying, I couldn't seem to find it in me to care. "Is he single?"

"Gabe..."

"Is he?"

"I don't know. No one knows. He's locked up tighter than the Fortress of Solitude."

Ah, okay, now I got his amusement from my earlier reference. "Is he straight? Gay?"

"I have no idea. I don't talk to him, and certainly not about that." Ryan rubbed at his forehead. "One thing I do know—this is a terrible idea."

It might've been, but that had never stopped me before. I was here to celebrate, to *enjoy* myself, and if a big fish was what I needed to be to get an introduction to *that* man, then a big fish I would become.

But first, I needed another drink.

CHAPTER 4

MARCUS

I WAS BORED. Truth be told, I'd been bored ten minutes into this thing, and now that an hour had passed, I would've paid just about anything to leave. That wasn't an option, though, since I was the one hosting this function, so for now I was taking a timeout.

I'd made my rounds earlier, making the usual small talk here and there with those I felt I should make an appearance with. But unfortunately for me, Alexander and Sean had left already to head back to their lakeside home, which meant the only two people I remotely considered "friends" were no longer here.

I moved away from the groups of people gathered and found a spot that I felt gave enough distance without being overly rude, and then gave myself a minute to just...be.

Despite my job title and position at ENN, I didn't enjoy all the pomp and circumstance that came with it. Award ceremonies, sponsor dinners, press hobnobbing in any capacity—it always felt like such an effort on my part. I'd much rather spend my time in a place without people who were constantly in my ear, needing something from me.

That was one of the reasons I'd much rather be at the symphony tonight. Once you got inside and the lights dimmed, all human interaction ceased and the music took over. That was definitely more my scene.

I stared out at the lights of downtown Chicago and was, as always, taken in by the sheer beauty of the city before me. This side of the building overlooked the sprawling metropolis below, whereas my office had views of Lake Michigan.

Either way was a winner in my opinion. Chicago might not be for everyone, but having been born and raised here, I had a deep-rooted love affair with the place that had yet to be matched elsewhere.

"Uh, excuse me? Hi there. Are you Marcus?"

I bit back a groan at the intrusion on my space, and wondered what part of my demeanor had invited this person to come and talk to me. It was clear that I hadn't wanted to be disturbed, since I'd purposely turned my back on the room. But still, here this man was, going out of his way to make small talk where it wasn't wanted.

I turned to see who'd dared to be so bold, and the face that greeted me had my icy reply instantly thawing. The man was stunning. Absolutely breathtaking. There were no two ways about it.

Eyes the color of polished amber and hair a rich chestnut, with tawny highlights. The hint of a five o'clock shadow against the copper tone of his skin showcased an angular jaw that was both elegant and masculine at the same time. It also emphasized a full set of lips that brought to mind sex and sin, and in that moment, I wanted both with him.

"You *are* Marcus, aren't you?"

I found it difficult to believe that anyone standing in this room—hell, this building—didn't know who I was. But that was his claim.

"I am. And you are?"

"Oh, sorry." He chuckled. "I'm one of your guests here tonight, and, uh, a friend of yours asked me to bring you over this drink."

That was a lie if ever I'd heard one. But I found myself pushing that aside for a chance to keep him talking. He was the most interesting thing that had happened to me all night, and I wasn't quite done with him yet.

"You're definitely not one of my guests. I never forget a face. As for friends, I don't have any of those. So, how about we try this again?"

I took a step in his direction. He didn't back up but instead grinned like a fiend, the two cheeky dimples bracketing his lips making him even more devastating to the eye.

"I'm Marcus, and you are?"

He glanced over his shoulder, and I couldn't stop myself from taking in the relaxed fit of his black jacket and open shirt. He'd left enough buttons free that it exposed him to mid-sternum, revealing smooth skin that looked warm to the touch, and a silver chain hung around his neck like a tease.

One that beckoned me to come closer and play with the shiny object in front of me.

But before I gave in to the impulse, he turned his attention back to me and held out the drink he'd used as a ruse to approach me in the first place.

"I'm Logan. Logan Mitchell."

Logan…

I definitely didn't know anyone by that name, and I knew everyone who worked here, so it was clear he was someone's plus-one. The question was, what was he doing over here if he'd arrived with someone else?

I reached for the drink he offered and studied the contents. It seemed Logan had a good eye. "A dirty martini?"

"As dirty as gets. That seemed like something you might like."

I had to hand it to him—this Logan had confidence in spades. No one in this building would ever dare talk to me the way he was right now, and the aggressive way he was coming onto me was…hot.

"It is, but I'm curious. How did you know what I was drinking?"

"I saw you hand off your glass earlier and took a wild guess." He raised his drink to his lips and took a sip. "I like it dirty too."

That wasn't surprising, especially with the shameless way he was flirting with me. It should've had me walking in the opposite direction, but instead it was drawing me in. Exciting me.

"Okay, you have my attention."

"I do, don't I?"

Yes, he fucking did, and yet I knew next to nothing about him. His name, that was it. And I suddenly found myself wanting to know more.

"Who did you come with tonight?"

A wicked grin tugged at the corner of his lips. "No one, yet. But the night's still young."

And so was he, if I had to guess. It was difficult to get a read on him, but I was thinking mid- to late twenties. Young enough to be confident, and old enough to know how to use it.

"You like playing games, Logan?"

"Depends. What's the game?"

"Right now? 'Hard to get' comes to mind."

He licked at his lower lip, and it was like a shot of adrenaline to my blood. "You're half right. Want to guess which half?"

A quick look down his body answered that question, his tailored pants doing little to hide the hard-on inside them. "Who did you come to the party with tonight?"

"No one important."

"Not a spouse?"

"Not a spouse." His gaze fell to my mouth and lingered. "Not a boyfriend, either, just in case you were wondering."

"I wasn't."

"Yes you were. Because I want to know the same thing about you."

"If I have a boyfriend?"

"Or anyone else who's going to ruin my chances here."

I took a sip of my drink and eyed him over the rim of my glass. "The only thing I'm attached to is my work. So unless you count that—"

"I definitely don't."

"That was quick." It wasn't often that I came across someone who wasn't one hundred percent career driven, so I was curious. "What is it that you do for a living?"

He took another sip of his drink, a longer one this time, and I had the sudden urge to kiss my way down his throat and between his open shirt. "I'm a lawyer."

That explained the confidence. But before I could ask him more, Logan reached for the swizzle stick in my drink and brought it to his lips. Then he sucked the olive off the end, chewed it, and swallowed.

"Mmm, nice and salty. I love that, don't you?"

CHAPTER 5

GABE

WHAT THE HELL was I doing? Not to mention *saying* to this guy?

I'd lost my mind. That was my only excuse. But come on, look at him. What else was I supposed to do? From the second I spotted him across the room, something inside me had sparked, and like the fuse of a firecracker, I'd watched it slowly burn a path from me to him until he finally turned around and—BOOM.

If I'd thought him compelling in his self-imposed isolation, up close, he was absolutely magnetic. A good couple of inches taller than myself, Marcus was at least six three, if I had to guess. His hair and closely cut beard were thick and golden in color—like sunshine—but that was where the warmth ended, because his cool and calculating stare took over, and something about that icy exterior made me want to chip away at it.

"You're very forward, considering we just met. Or is that a lawyer thing?"

It definitely wasn't, since, well, I wasn't a lawyer. But there was no way in hell someone like him would ever look twice at a guy who'd just dropped out of university. So, I'd decided to take on the persona of someone he wouldn't be able to resist—my new boss.

Yes, I'd fudged the facts a little, but it wasn't like I was looking for a long-term thing here. I was looking for one night to have a good time, and I wanted to have it with him.

"Maybe. Or it could just be that I saw something I wanted and decided to come and get it."

A flash of fire illuminated Marcus's cool eyes, and they turned an intense blue. It was brief, a couple seconds at the most, but it was enough to have my blood humming.

"And is that what you think you're doing? *Getting* me?"

"I'm trying."

Marcus took the empty glass from me and handed it off to a passing waiter, then he lowered his gaze over me and said in a voice that had my pulse racing, "Try harder."

Now *that* was a green light if ever I'd heard one. "Here?"

Marcus's lips curled in the hint of a smile, and my eyes immediately fell to them. In fact, I was finding it incredibly difficult to look anywhere else. I loved his beard. It covered his chiseled jaw and firm lips, and I knew I'd do whatever the hell he wanted me to if I meant I got to taste them by the end of the night.

"Why not? You just said you were coming to get me. So...get me."

Oh shit. Okay. Think, Gabe, think.

So far, I'd gambled that someone like him would be drawn to confidence and assertiveness, and clearly that had worked—then I remembered... "You have an office on this floor, don't you?"

Marcus raised an eyebrow. "I don't know, do I?"

"That's what I was told."

"Is that right? And what else were you told, Logan?"

The use of my pseudo-name pulled me out of my fantasy for a second, but I quickly recovered. I wasn't proud of myself for the deception, but at least my next words were true: "That you're out of my league."

Marcus's eyes narrowed, and he looked out to the crowd as though trying to decide who had told me that, then he took *another* step toward me until we were so close that the tips of our shoes practically touched.

"Whoever said that, I'll fire them tomorrow."

I knew he was joking, but the promise was sexy as fuck. *Sorry, Ryan.*

"My office—"

"Yes?"

"It's the only other room on this floor. Why don't you think of a good reason to go and wait for me outside of it and I'll show it to you, if you like?"

If I liked? I would *love* to see his office. Preferably his desk, up close and personal, when I was stretched out over it.

"And what are you going to do while I go and wait?"

"I have to congratulate my employees on a job well done. But then, I'm going to come and get *you*."

A shiver of anticipation raced up my spine as he took a step back.

"It was very nice to meet you, Logan." Marcus slipped his hands into his pockets and moved around me. "I hope to see much more of you...soon."

As he walked off toward the podium, I turned to watch him go, and I was again held hostage by the commanding way he filled a space. Apparently, I wasn't the only one, because the second Marcus was behind the microphone, all talking in the room ceased, and the crowd gathered in close to one another and moved toward the front of the room.

It was the perfect opportunity for me to slip to the back of the crowd, and when I finally reached the double doors, Marcus's deep voice filled the room.

"Good evening, everyone, and thank you for coming tonight..." His eyes found mine across the room for a moment, and if there'd been any doubt in my mind, it slipped right out the door only seconds before I did.

CHAPTER 6

MARCUS

WHEN I STEPPED out of the conference room and spotted Logan leaning up against the wall by my office door, I knew what I was about to do was a mistake. I never did this kind of thing, and I especially didn't do it with a complete stranger. But when he turned in my direction and my pulse spiked, I knew nothing in the world—save this building catching on fire—would stop me from going to him.

It'd been a long time since I'd been drawn to someone this way, and as I walked toward him and he pushed off the wall to watch my approach, that hum of anticipation began all over again.

Jesus, he was easy on the eyes. Unlike any of the other men at the party tonight, he was the epitome of cool and casual, and it worked for him. With the open shirt and peek at the bronze skin against the stark white material, he gave the appearance of someone who enjoyed kicking back and enjoying an afternoon in the sun.

A silver bracelet adorned his left wrist, and I wondered if it matched the chain around his neck. I made a mental note to make sure I got close enough to him again tonight to get another look at it.

When I stopped opposite him, I slipped my hands into my pockets to make sure I didn't shove him back against my office wall. I couldn't remember the last time I'd felt so out of control. So reckless.

"You waited," I said.

"I did. But I was starting to think you'd sent me out here just to play with me."

A devilish smile curved Logan's lips, and when those dimples reappeared, they gave a mischievous edge that was a killer combination. He had a face that was difficult to look away from, and now that no one else was around, I was done feigning indifference.

"Isn't that what you want? Me to play with you?"

He licked along his lush bottom lip, and I was curious how far he was willing to take this. It'd been a hell of a long time since I'd had a one-time hookup, but there was something about him that wouldn't let me walk away.

"Among other things," he said.

"Such as?"

"Hmm, well..." Bold as ever, he placed his hand on the lapel of my jacket and tested the material beneath his palm. "You were going to show me your office, weren't you?"

I looked to the closed door and then back down the hall

where there was a conference room full of people, and decided I wanted him somewhere less...populated.

"I don't know. If you've seen one office, you've seen them all. Am I right?"

Logan's hand froze, and I could tell he thought he'd pushed too far. But that wasn't the problem at all. The real issue here was that I wanted to push this all the way.

"Have you ever seen a news studio before?"

That flirty smirk from earlier returned in an instant. He cocked his head and sized me up. "You did that on purpose, didn't you?"

"What's that?"

"Fucked with me."

I chuckled as I stepped around him. "Trust me, you'll know when I'm doing that with you. I told you, right now, I'm playing with you."

I walked by him, and Logan turned and kept pace beside me as we headed toward the elevators. "Sooo, you're going to give me a...tour?"

I pushed the down button, and when the elevator door immediately opened, I gestured inside. "Yes. A very personal one."

His lips twitched as he walked inside, leaned back against the wall, and gave me a not-so-subtle once-over. "And? Do I pass inspection?"

"You know you do." I couldn't help but notice how thick his dark lashes were. "I haven't been able to stop looking at you since I saw you."

"That works both ways. It's nice to finally be able to look with no one else around."

"Feel free to look...closer."

I zeroed in on his mouth and took a step forward, more than ready to do just that. But before I did something crazy where there were cameras at all angles, the elevator *dinged*, saving me from myself.

Logan grinned. "Saved by the bell?"

"For the moment," I said as we moved out of the elevator.

It was quiet down here now. The late-night news broadcast from the studio upstairs, and as I led Logan inside the main newsroom, he stopped and looked around at the wide-open space.

There were desks everywhere, televisions on the walls, and clocks with the times from all the major U.S. cities, and international ones too. Offices lined the perimeter of the mammoth space, and over on the far side of the room were the doors that led into the two control rooms and studios. It was impressive even in its dormant state.

"Wow. So this is where it all happens."

"It is." I led him through the rabbit warren of desks. "During the day it's a madhouse in here, but these studios shut down by ten each night. The late-night programs are filmed one floor up."

When I reached the other side of the room, I turned, expecting to see him taking it all in. Instead, he was looking directly at me.

"So what you're trying to say"—he crossed the distance between us, and the tension in the air crackled with enough energy to power every device in the room—"is that no one else is here right now?"

When he stopped in front of me, I clenched my hands inside my pockets in an effort not to reach out and touch the sharp angle of his chin. But I promised myself that by the end of the night I would measure its lines and test its stubbled texture with my lips and mouth instead.

"No one, save a couple dozen security cameras."

"Ah..." Logan looked over my shoulder and up to the corners of the expansive room, then brought his attention back to me. "And whoever's at the other end of these cameras—"

"Larry."

Logan bit his lip, and I had the distinct impression he was trying not to laugh at me. "*Larry*. Would he be scandalized to see you in here kissing another man?"

There was that confidence again. That no-holds-barred attitude that was so different to all the other men who usually approached me. I was so used to the scheming of the timid that I'd forgotten what a turn-on it was to be so brazenly chased.

"I believe he would be, yes." I leaned forward a fraction and placed my mouth by his ear. "The real question is, would I care?"

Logan turned his head so our noses all but touched, and his golden eyes were practically glowing.

"Would you like to see the control room?"

His low chuckle made my cock ache. "That sounds kinky."

"Maybe in some circles." I straightened to my full height. "Here, it's just an everyday norm."

"I'm sure it is in their circles too."

I smiled as I headed off toward the studio doors, and as he followed closely behind, I could feel his attention as tangible as a touch.

"Behind that door is Studio A, and on the other side, Studio B. Hair and makeup is over there, and this"—I pushed open the door—"is Control Room A."

Logan moved ahead of me and let out a low whistle. The TV monitors were all shut down for the night. But the rows of control panels, microphones, headsets, and the vast array of other equipment needed to produce the nightly news sat waiting to do its job come morning.

"This place is impressive." Logan walked down the center aisle toward the monitors and looked around. "You never think about everything that goes on behind the scenes when you sit down to watch live television. But this is where all the last-minute decisions are made, aren't they?"

"That's right," I said as I drank in the sight of him, the width of his shoulders, his trim waist outlined by his jacket, and I wanted to see more. "Obviously we go in with a game plan, the news that has happened throughout the day. But if anything breaks while we're on air, this is where it comes first. The EP—executive producer—makes sure it's been verified and edited down. One of the guys will get graphics together, and within a matter of minutes, sometimes seconds, the anchor is told what's going on and fed the new information during the break or while on air."

Logan glanced over his shoulder at me. "Sounds exciting."

"It can be. It can also be very stressful making sure that all the facts are correct. That what you're about to tell millions of people is the truth."

"And that's important to you?" Logan said as he walked back up the aisle to me.

"My job depends on it, so yes. You'd be the same in that sense, I imagine, with your clients. They have to swear under oath, and a lot of what you do depends on being told the truth."

"Right, yes, that's true. But we also tend to fudge the facts a little to get to the things we want."

"I can imagine."

"Can you?"

"Yes. Sometimes we have to bend the rules in order to get the information we need."

"And tonight?" Logan daringly reached for the end of my tie and stroked it between his fingers. "Are you bending the rules for me?"

"I think you already know that I am."

He slicked his tongue along his lower lip. "I like that."

So did my throbbing dick. I placed my hand over the top of his. "Come with me."

Without a word, I led him out of the control room, down the hall, and into Studio A. If he was impressed by what he saw, he didn't say so. Instead, he followed silently, understanding that I was leading him to a place where we could finally explore what had been building between us from that first moment back in the conference room.

With the main lights shut off and only the security lights illuminating the space, the cameras, spotlights, and booms cast shadows all around the studio. But I knew where every security camera was pointed, and the one spot that was blind was the south wall of Studio A.

I drew Logan into the shadowy corner, and when I turned to see him looking at me with hooded eyes, I had a flash of him in my bed with his eyes closed and those thick lashes kissing the top curve of his cheek.

The image was so real, so potent, and so fucking sexy that I was moving before I even realized what I was doing. I had his back against the wall, and I finally gave in to the one thing I'd wanted since I turned around and saw him standing in front of me—I touched him.

I traced my fingers down his cheek and over the stubble, and the rough scratch beneath my fingertips made my already interested cock harden in response. Logan clutched at the lapels of my jacket and angled his face up toward mine.

Fuck. He must've woven some kind of magic over me tonight, because all I could think about was stripping him naked and burying myself so deep inside him that I'd be lost for days. As it was, I'd have to settle for fast and quick, because there were no guarantees on how long we'd be alone.

With that thought in mind, I took his chin in my hand, then lowered my head and whispered against his lips, "Got you."

CHAPTER 7
GABE

ONE OF MY favorite things in life was a first kiss. There was something so special about them. Something so telling about the kind of experience you were about to have, and judging by this one, I was in for a hell of a ride.

I'd known it was going to be good, or at least, I had high hopes it would be. But when Marcus touched me, the fire that had started upstairs ignited into a blazing inferno, and I had to curl my fingers into his jacket just so I wouldn't melt at his feet.

His lips were firm and warm as he brushed them along the top of mine. But when he nipped at my lower lip for access and I gave it, things went from zero to sixty in the blink of an eye.

Marcus's tongue entered with arrogance, sweeping the interior of my mouth and exploring every inch of it. When a growl rumbled from the back of his throat, I angled my head to give him better access.

He took immediate advantage, cradling my face between his hands, then he continued to devour me one savage kiss at a time. I smoothed my palms down his lapels and under his jacket to his ass, as he continued to obliterate every single one of my senses. Marcus thrust his hips forward, and when his erection came into contact with mine, I tore my mouth free and let out a curse.

Hellbent on destroying my control, however, Marcus kissed his way down the side of my throat. His fingers followed the same path, trailing down to my open shirt, where he hooked his finger around the silver chain of my necklace.

It was a simple gesture, but when he began to slide his finger back and forth along the metal, my dick began to pulse.

"I promised myself I'd get close enough to look at this before I let you go tonight." He glanced down at the small pendant of a heart—a very *unique* heart—that I'd been given years ago. He narrowed his eyes as though trying to work it out, then let it go and added, "I also promised myself I'd do this."

He lowered his head and pressed several scorching kisses down the center of my chest, and I'd never been more thankful I'd ditched the tie and popped free the buttons of my shirt.

When he reached the point where the material finally covered me, he flicked his tongue out and then dragged it back up my body to the base of my throat. My head thunked back against the wall and Marcus raised his head.

Blue eyes blazed down at me and my body vibrated with need, then he reached between us and popped the button of my pants free. I sucked in a breath as the sound of my zipper echoed in the otherwise silent room, then he slipped his hand inside and fingered the elastic edge of my briefs.

"I don't do this kind of thing," he said as he slipped his fingers under the band. "I don't kiss strange men, bring them somewhere private, and then wonder how quickly I can get inside them. But with you, I can't seem to stop myself."

Somewhere in the back of my head, I'd already known that. There was something about him that screamed *private*, that emanated discretion, but that had been half his appeal.

Marcus was the sexiest man I'd ever met, and the added challenge of getting his attention—of making him *see* me—had been a combination I wasn't able to resist. When he lowered to his knees and tugged my pants and briefs down to mid-thigh, it was all I could do to stop myself from coming right there.

My cock was aching and hard, my arousal at fever pitch, as Marcus wrapped a hand around me and then raised his eyes to mine.

"You're not the only one who likes it salty."

"Oh *God*." I squeezed my eyes shut and took in a ragged breath, and just when I thought I might have some hope of regaining control of myself, Marcus leaned forward and flicked his tongue over the head of my dick.

I reached for him, threading my fingers through his blond hair, and yes, it was as soft as it was thick. But then I had a thought: "Aren't there...a lot of cameras in here?"

Marcus's hand tightened around the root of my cock. "There are."

"And that—*ah shit*—doesn't worry you?"

The sinful light in his eyes made a shiver race up my spine. "It would, if any were pointed in this direction."

Fucking hell, that was hot. The fact that he knew where the security cameras were and had pulled me somewhere private told me I was about to get exactly what I wanted from him, and I was more than ready.

"Still want to play?" he asked.

He grazed his thumb over the head of my erection, and a tortured moan left me. "Hell yes. I love games."

Marcus leaned forward and sucked the tip of my shaft between his lips.

I tightened my fingers in his hair, and my head fell back against the wall. Then he began to stroke up my length as his mouth slid down it, and I shoved forward as deep as I could go.

Marcus growled and swallowed me, taking me in and out of his hot, wet mouth, and when he finally pulled his lips free, he moved in close to nuzzle at the root of my dick.

"You smell and taste fucking amazing." His voice was rough like gravel, and when I tugged his head back, rubbing myself against his bearded cheek, the lust swirling in his eyes made my balls tighten.

How I'd ever thought him icy or cold, I had no idea, because the heat emanating off him now was damn near scorching. Marcus got to his feet and took my hand in his, tugging me off the wall.

He pressed a hard, brutal kiss to my lips, then spun me around and muscled me up against the unforgiving surface. I was so turned on at this point that it wasn't going to take all that much to get me to the finish line, but, not wanting to get there before him, I reached down and clamped my hand tight around myself.

Marcus crowded in behind me. The soft material of his suit pants brushing over my bare skin made me rest my forehead to the wall and count back from thirty. He placed a hand by my head and used his other to glide it over the round curve of my ass, then ran a finger down my cleft. I pushed back into the touch.

"I really wish I had longer to—"

"I know," I said, and looked back at him. "My wallet... I have something in my wallet."

Marcus's blond eyebrow arched, but I wasn't about to feel embarrassed. In fact, I was feeling the exact opposite. I was glad that I'd put that condom in there tonight. I'd wanted to celebrate, wanted to have a good time, and I wasn't about to let being unprepared get in my way if the right man came along.

And, well, the right man was definitely about to come along—with me.

Marcus reached into my pocket, and when he pulled my wallet out, I said, "It's in the card compartment on the back."

As he pulled the small packet free, I'd never been more thankful I hadn't put that sucker inside by my license. He slipped my wallet back in my pants, and the next thing I heard was the distinct sound of a belt clasp echoing around the room.

Jesus, this was hot, the hottest thing I'd ever done in my life. I was standing in a damn news studio with cameras everywhere, and in about ten seconds I was about to have the guy that ran the place inside me. My pulse was racing as my heart thumped in time with my throbbing cock. When Marcus's fingers once again found my bare skin, I clenched my teeth together in an effort not to end this all before it started. He followed the narrow channel of my ass up and down in a teasing motion that made my legs shake.

I could feel his warm breath on the back of my neck, and when he finally pushed his fingers a little deeper, he kissed his way up to my ear.

"This may be just one night, but I'm going to think about you for a very long time after this." His fingertip pressed against the place I wanted him most. "The way you look, the way you smell, the way your body will no doubt cling to mine when I fuck you right here against the studio wall..."

I groaned as he pulled his finger out and shoved it back inside.

"Then I'm going to get off thinking about the sounds you made when I touched you right here."

"*Ah.*" I clamped my hand around my cock as his finger found that magical spot. "Marcus."

"Damn, I like how that sounds way too fucking much," he said against the skin behind my ear, then he withdrew his finger and placed a hand on one of my cheeks, spreading me wide. "Think I can make you shout it?"

Yeah, I fucking did. At this point, I was completely shameless. If he wanted me to scream his name, then I'd scream it at the top of my lungs. I wasn't afraid to admit how much I wanted him. Hell, I was standing here with my pants down, begging him to get inside me.

Marcus's cock nudged at my entrance. He scraped his teeth down my neck to where the chain of my necklace lay, and I let out a cry and thrust back against him.

As the wide head of him breached the first tight ring of muscles, my entire body tensed, my toes curling in my shoes. But then he began to suck on the skin of my neck, and a delicious warmth spread throughout my body. My muscles relaxed.

He kissed and sucked his way up under my ear as he slid deeper inside me, and when he was as deep as he could go, he placed one hand on the wall and reached around me to take my stiff dick in the other.

I let my head fall back onto his shoulder and rolled my hips, sliding along his length. Marcus flexed his hand around my shaft and began to stroke. My eyes fell shut, and I reveled in this once-in-a-lifetime moment.

He fit me perfectly, touched me exactly where I needed him to, and when he moved us back to the wall and took one of my hands in his to brace it against the surface, I knew we were both close to the edge.

With my feet locked in place and Marcus's large frame engulfing me, I felt totally surrounded by him, and in that moment, I never wanted to leave. I closed my eyes and memorized every sound, feeling, and emotion I was experiencing. As he picked up the pace and my climax threatened, I curled my fingers with his and held on tight. The whirlwind we found ourselves in reached its terminal velocity, and Marcus tunneled deep one last time.

"Marcus," I shouted, and he cursed by my ear. Then I tensed in his arms and surrendered with a blissful kind of reluctance, as he nuzzled into my shoulder and whispered my name.

"Logan..."

Except it wasn't my name.

It shouldn't have mattered. I shouldn't have cared. This was one night, and Logan's persona had been my foot in the door. But as Marcus pulled out of me and our moment together came to its end, I couldn't help but think I'd just done myself a disservice.

I'd just met the man of my dreams, and as I slipped out his arms and, not long after that, out his life, I realized he would forever be dreaming about a man who wasn't me.

CHAPTER 8

MARCUS

THE HUSTLE AND bustle of the morning commuters accompanied me as I made my way down the sidewalk to the high-rise building where today's morning meeting was.

It was just coming up on nine fifteen, and I was early. I'd agreed to meet Gloria at this new law office, since she would be coming straight from home and I was coming from ENN, but the idea of waiting for anyone made me itchy. I wasn't one for lingering, and I had a million things that needed to be done today. So I was hoping to wrap this meeting up quickly.

I pushed through the lobby doors and made my way across the marble floors to the elevator banks. Several stores dotted the outskirts of the lower level, including a bustling café that was serving up caffeine to whoever needed the hit, and a bar, from the looks of it—After Hours.

It was closed right now, but it was one of those fancy

corporate hangouts where meetings were held, deals were made, and a bad day could vanish at the bottom of a glass tumbler.

Personally, I preferred unwinding on my own with a glass of scotch and some classical music. That way there was no outside noise, no one who wanted or needed anything from me.

I hit the button on the elevator and had a sudden flash of the striking face that had captivated me last week—Logan. Now there was someone I wouldn't mind wanting something from me.

I'd thought about him, and that night, a lot over the past six days. Yes, the fact that I'd kept track of how many days it had been since we'd met wasn't lost on me. Nor was the fact that I couldn't stop thinking about him.

It was distracting and completely pointless, since I was never going to see him again. Judging by the way he'd managed to take up residence in my head after such a brief encounter, it was probably for the best that he was long gone.

When the elevator doors opened, I stepped inside and shoved aside all thoughts other than why I was here. Gloria had invited me here today for a very specific reason, and my cheery disposition was not it.

She wanted a second set of eyes and ears when she was given this latest pitch. She wanted an unbiased, outside opinion, from a person who wasn't pissed off that their current law firm was trying to screw them. Gloria wanted to know if I would entrust my—our—staff members to these people. That they would ultimately go to bat for our staff, and in the end, win. I wanted that too. But I also didn't want to sit through some over-the-top presentation of all the reasons we should pick these guys as ENN's new law firm.

When the elevator reached the corporate floor for the firm and opened, I stepped into an exquisite lobby that was impressive to say the least. Straight ahead of me was the reception desk, which was made out of rich woods and shiny marble, and directly behind the young lady who clearly reigned supreme over her territory was a mottled glass divider that read, *Mitchell & Madison Attorneys at Law*.

I made my way across the polished floors and past the waiting room to the left, and unfortunately, no Gloria. Although that was probably for the best. If these guys wanted to take on the largest broadcasting network in the U.S., it probably wouldn't be smart to let its CEO sit in the waiting room. No matter how nice it might be.

"Hello. Welcome to Mitchell & Madison. How can I help you this morning?"

"Hello. My name is Marcus St. James. I'm with Tennant Broadcasting. Gloria Tennant and I have a meeting today at nine thirty."

"Of course." Tiffany—her name badge said—smiled and typed something into her computer. She nodded and gestured to the waiting area. "If you'd like to take a seat, I'll let them know you're here."

"Thank you."

I grabbed one of their business cards and then took a seat, where I pulled my phone out to check for any emails, messages, or calls I might've missed. When there was nothing that needed my immediate attention, I opened the ENN app and checked out this morning's news.

I scrolled through, reading the major stories, then flicked to stocks and the economy, before deciding to see when the next date was for the Chicago Symphony. The last performance had been a little over a month ago, and I was looking forward to seeing when their next showcase would be. This Saturday. I quickly made a note in my calendar and made sure to keep it free. Then I slipped my phone into the interior pocket of my jacket and settled in to wait.

Not five minutes later, I heard the distinct sound of leather shoes on marble floors, and looked up in time to see a man dressed in a sharp black suit step around the corner.

I recognized him in an instant. The rich chestnut hair that was still a little tousled, but much more tamed than the night I'd had my hands in it. The perfect stubble lining a sharp jaw line that I'd licked and sucked before I took his lips in a fiery kiss. And those eyes, those warm amber eyes, that widened now as they landed on me.

Logan? How in the hell—

"What is it that you do for a living?"

"I'm a lawyer."

Shit.

If there was one thing I never did, it was mix business and pleasure. As I got to my feet and Logan's eyes swept over me, my cock made it crystal clear which one of those two categories it put this man in.

There was no way I was heading into a meeting with

him. Gloria would have to do this on her own. I could make up an excuse to leave. Have an issue down at the station. Anything to get me out this situation where me and my dick had potentially muddied the waters on a deal.

Or had it?

I took a second look at the business card in my hand and the two names underneath the company's logo—Logan Mitchell and Cole Madison—and that was when a much more alarming thought took root.

Had Logan purposely sought me out that night believing it would make a difference in whether we hired them? He *was* one of the partners here. One of the owners. Although he seemed far too young for that. I'd thought of him as a fresh-out-of-law-school lawyer. Not part owner. But maybe he came from money? I didn't know, and that was beginning to piss me off.

Because if he thought that night was going to win him any favors here, he was in for a rude awakening.

Logan cleared his throat and took a step toward me, then held his hand out for me to shake, as though I'd never pinned it against a wall while I buried myself inside him.

"Good morning," he said, and swallowed when I took his hand in mine. "You must be Mr. St. James."

At the complete lack of acknowledgment of our acquaintance, I narrowed my eyes and could've sworn I saw a flash of panic.

"Well, aren't we formal this morning?" I said.

Logan pulled his hand free and glanced over his shoulder as though making sure no one had heard me.

His black suit was much more proper than the one he'd worn last week, as was his neatly buttoned shirt and perfectly tied tie, and the black leather shoes were polished so well that I could practically see my reflection in them.

I couldn't believe he was standing in front of me, and judging by the jumpy way he was behaving, he couldn't believe it either.

Which had me wondering: "Did you know who I was that night in the conference room? That I had a business meeting at your firm today?"

Logan quickly shook his head. "*No.* No. I had no idea, and—" A frown creased his brow as he stopped talking, then he seemed to regroup and started up again. "If you'll follow me, I'll take you somewhere that we can discuss—"

"I don't think so. I don't mix business with my personal life, and despite the way you're behaving, we got very personal last Friday."

Logan grimaced, but then he took another step closer and lowered his voice so only I could hear. "Marcus, please. Give me a chance to explain."

While everything in my head shouted, *Leave now and let Gloria deal with this,* I couldn't deny the way my body reacted when he said my name like that.

This man affected me. He had the first time we met, and he was right now, and no matter how foolish it might be, I wasn't quite ready to walk away from him yet.

"You've got five minutes."

"Okay." Logan licked his full bottom lip and then gestured for me to follow him. "Five minutes."

CHAPTER 9
GABE

FIVE *MINUTES?* I'D be lucky if I didn't get fired in the next two.

Shit. Shit. Shit. What is Marcus doing here?

When I stepped out to meet Logan's client and bring him back for the morning meeting, I'd been told it was with the CEO of Tennant Broadcasting, not the president of ENN Worldwide. How was I supposed to know the two were connected? I'd never expected to see Marcus again, let alone here.

This was bad, about as bad as it could get. Here I was a week into one of the best jobs I'd ever had, and I was about to blow it because I'd lied to one of the most important men in Chicago.

Not only lied, but told him that I was Logan—my *boss*—who was about to show up any moment now and realize he'd made the biggest mistake of his life in hiring me.

Ugh, I was in so much trouble that I didn't even know

where to start. But one thing I did know was that five minutes wasn't going to cut it. Hell, I'd be lucky if I could even tell Marcus my real *name* by the time I found somewhere private.

I led him down the U-shaped hall that surrounded our meeting space, and for the first time since I'd started work at Mitchell & Madison, I hated the modern look of the glass-walled conference room.

What I wouldn't do for a room with no windows and no view right now, so I could take Marcus in there, tell him the truth, and then die of humiliation in private. But it appeared I was out of luck.

I pushed open the door to the room and thanked my lucky stars that a) it was empty for now, and b) it was soundproof. Maybe I could get this over and done with before Logan discovered what I'd done and fired me on the spot. I mean, really, this was going to be embarrassing enough without losing every ounce of dignity I had.

As I stepped inside and turned, I was again brought up short by just how damn attractive Marcus was. His thick hair was styled off to the right, and his beard was trimmed nice and short, making me think of the way it had felt against my skin the other night. His grey suit hugged his broad shoulders, and with the white shirt and striped tie to match, he looked professional, powerful, and one hundred percent pissed off.

He also looked about two seconds away from blasting me with that icy tone he'd used out in the lobby. He probably thought that was intimidating, and to most it probably was, but to me it just made him all the more appealing, because I knew just how hot he could get once that ice thawed.

"Logan? Do you want to tell me what the hell is going on?"

I moved behind one of the chairs around the large oval table and tried to think of the best way to start. How did you tell someone that you'd lied to get their attention and that you weren't really who you said you were? I had no idea. And the longer I stood there thinking, the worse it all sounded in my head. *This* was a nightmare, and just when I thought it couldn't get any worse, Logan stepped out of his office and began walking in our direction.

Think, Gabe, think. But there was no time, and as Logan pushed open the conference room door, I said the first thing that came to mind and hoped by some miracle of God he took pity on me and my pathetic self.

"*Cole,*" I announced. Logan's brow furrowed. I plastered a false smile on my face and thought, *You're in it now, Gabe. Fake it till he fires you.* "This is Marcus St. James, who's here for *our* meeting this morning. Marcus, this is Cole Madison, my brother and one of my other partners here at the firm."

A suspicious light entered Logan's eyes as the door to the conference room slowly shut behind him, then he pivoted to face Marcus. But before either man could say anything, I quickly added, "I was just helping him settle in."

Logan eyed me from behind his black frames, and this time his expression said one thing: *Stop. Talking.* I sent up a quick prayer that whatever punishment he decided to deliver to me be quick, painless, and preferably anywhere but here, and then I waited for him to decide my fate.

"Good morning. Sorry I wasn't out there to greet you with my"—Logan looked my way, and I held my breath—"*brother*. I got caught up on the phone, and I apologize."

I let out a silent sigh of relief as Logan walked over to me. God only knew what he was thinking right now.

"No apologies necessary," Marcus replied. "Logan showed me in here as soon as I arrived."

"Did he now?"

I couldn't stop myself from glancing at my boss, and he looked...amused. The exact opposite to what I'd expected to see.

"Yes. However, I just got called back to the newsroom, so I won't be able to stay. Not that that's of any consequence, since Gloria is the one who makes the decisions anyway."

It was official: I was frozen solid. But luckily for me, I had an unflappable lawyer standing beside me.

"That's a shame," Logan said. "Maybe we'll have a chance to catch up later?"

The expression on Marcus's face said that that was highly unlikely, but Logan didn't seem bothered at all. He stepped forward and held out his hand.

"It was nice to meet you, Marcus."

"You too...Cole." Marcus reached for Logan's hand and shook it. Then his eyes cut to me where I stood paralyzed. "Logan."

Oh God, just kill me now.

I nodded because it was all I could seem to do, then

watched in complete silence as Marcus walked out the door. When he finally disappeared out into the lobby, I braved a look in my boss's direction. He was standing with his arms crossed and an expectant look on his face.

"So, would you like to try to *explain* what just happened now, or should I just guess?"

I opened my mouth to try to deliver *some* kind of explanation, but when no words came out, I quickly shut it again.

"Okay," Logan said as he rubbed his fingers against his jaw. "Let's go with this, shall we? At the end of this meeting today, you are to go over to Tennant Broadcasting, get yourself a meeting with that man, and explain to him *whatever* it is you have done."

"But I—"

"*That* is what you are going to do if you want to keep this job. It's obvious he's important to this decision, no matter what he just said. But for reasons I do not know, he just left because of something *I* supposedly did. Fix this, Gabe. Or you're gone. Do I make myself clear?"

My cheeks flamed. I knew I deserved it. I deserved much worse. I quickly nodded, and when one of the phone lines lit up, I thanked God that I now had something to do other than stand there and wish I could disappear.

I reached for the receiver and listened intently as Tiffany informed me that Gloria Tennant was there, then I hung up and told Logan I would go and get her.

I'd just pulled open the glass door to leave when I heard, "Oh, and Gabe?"

I turned back to see Logan with the phone in his hand, probably about to call in Mr. Madison and Mr. Priestley.

"Yes?"

"From here on out, you're my bitch. Got it?" His smirk made my anxiety ease a little. I stepped outside of the conference room and let out a deep breath.

Okay, so at least he hadn't fired me on the spot. Now all I had to do was find a way to get Marcus to see me later today, which seemed like the most impossible task in the world, since he'd all but run out of here in an effort to do the exact opposite of that.

CHAPTER 10
GABE

IT WAS NEARLY two hours later that I found myself standing on the sidewalk in front of the ENN building, wondering what the hell I was doing there.

There was no way Marcus was going to see me, not after the way things had gone down at Mitchell & Madison, and that was when he thought I'd somehow lured him to the meeting in the first place. Wait until he found out I wasn't who I'd said I was.

That was going to go over well.

But Logan had been clear: don't come back unless I could fix this, and since I'd screwed up in the first place, the least I could do was try to right this wrong before my life fell completely apart.

Maybe I could at least salvage Logan's reputation with Marcus. After all, it wasn't like *he'd* had a one-night stand with him. As for me, I had a feeling that by the end of this day I'd be unemployed and one hundred percent humiliated.

I sighed, resigned to my fate, and headed inside the building. I punched the number to the floor the party had been held on last week, and waited for the doors to close. I leaned back against the wall and had a flash of Marcus as he'd stood in front of me that night and offered to give me a personal tour of the newsroom, and God I wished things were different.

I'd never been so attracted to someone in my life, and while I'd almost convinced myself it was because it was all so illicit and spontaneous, when I saw him again this morning, I knew that for the lie it was.

It was because it was Marcus, a man I barely even knew, and yet I was more drawn to him standing in a lobby with him glaring daggers at me than I'd ever been to anybody else before. That instant BOOM was still there. Like a bolt of lightning.

When the elevator came to his floor and the doors opened, I hoped I wouldn't run into Ryan anywhere along the way, because really, that was all I would need to round this day out.

I stepped into the lobby and made my way down the hall, and, unlike last week, found a woman sitting behind the reception desk. She looked up as I approached, and I had to remind myself how to speak.

Shit. I needed to pull it together if I had a hope in hell of talking my way into a meeting with a man who was likely booked until next year.

"Good morning," she said when I finally came to a stop in front of her. "Can I help you with something?"

"Yes, um, I need to speak to Mr. St. James, if he has a moment."

The expression on her face told me that was a no before she even got the words out.

"Mr. St. James is in meetings all morning. If you leave me your name and number, and what it is you need, I can check his schedule with him and set up an appointment."

That wasn't going to work for me, since there was no way he'd call *Logan* back, and, well, he didn't know a Gabe. So my only option here was to be sneaky.

"Really, I just need a couple minutes of his time."

"Unfortunately, he doesn't have a couple of minutes to spare. Again, if you would just leave me your name and—"

"Okay, a couple of seconds. I'd take a couple of seconds." Yes, I was being persistent, but desperate times called for desperate measures.

"*Sir.* Mr. St. James is currently on a conference call. After that, he has meetings lined up back to back. He cannot be—"

That was all I needed to know. I was halfway down the hall and making a beeline for Marcus's office before the lady had a chance to even round her desk. I knew what I was about to do was stupid and reckless, and hardly the way to win back points. But what other option did I have?

I gave two swift knocks on what I knew was Marcus's office door, opened it without waiting for a reply, and slipped inside. I quickly shut it and leaned back against the wooden surface, as a frantic knock sounded behind me. I grimaced and looked over my shoulder as though I'd see the woman through the door, but instead noticed a lock on the handle and flicked it into place.

I let out a sigh and spotted Marcus sitting behind his enormous desk with his eyes locked on me like a laser beam.

"Mr. Chen," Marcus said, without taking his eyes off me. "I'm sorry to do this, but something's come up that I have to deal with. Do you mind if I call you back at the same time tomorrow?"

"Of course not. We'll pick this up then."

"Perfect. Until tomorrow."

Marcus sat forward and pressed a button on his phone. Then he sat back in his seat and slowly looked me over from head to toe.

Shit. What is he thinking? I had no idea, but when the knocking on the door sounded again, I startled and Marcus arched an eyebrow.

"I assume that's Carmen pounding on my door right now?"

I looked over my shoulder at the door and then back to him. "If Carmen sits behind the desk in the lobby and guards every second on your schedule as though her life depends on it... Then yes, that's who's pounding on your door."

Marcus's eyes narrowed, and while most would probably find that look intimidating, I found myself attracted to it. I pushed away from the door and walked into the center of his office, and for the first time since I'd burst inside, I took a moment to look around.

It was massive, just like the conference room, and decorated in similar shades of blues and greys. But where those windows overlooked downtown Chicago, Marcus had a beautiful view of the lake.

A wall of bookcases sat at one end of the office, and couches lined the wall facing the windows. As I continued toward Marcus, I noted a matching bookcase behind him that housed photos, awards, and, yes, even a couple of books.

The office was sleek and elegant, like the man himself, and everything about it screamed that Marcus was one hell of a big deal around here—just in case you didn't know.

"Is there a reason you've just interrupted a call between me and the new president of ENN Shanghai, or are you just here to collect on the tour you missed out on last week?"

Oh yeah, Marcus was pissed. His tone was clipped, his shoulders rigid, and I could tell by the harsh set of his jaw that his teeth were clenched. This wasn't going to end well for me, but in for a penny, in for a pound. I just needed to suck it up and do it.

"I'm actually here to talk about what happened this morning."

Marcus arched an eyebrow. "This morning?"

"Okay, not *only* this morning, but I need to start with that first." I gestured to a seat. "May I?"

"You just barged in here unannounced, interrupted an important phone call, and now you're concerned with my wishes?"

He had a point, so with that, I sat down. As I did, I noticed the close way he watched me, and I was reminded of a lion. He had that still and silent way about him, as though he had all the time in the world to sit there and wait for his prey to make a wrong move—but he wasn't going to have to wait that long.

"There's really no good way to start this—"

"Then how about you just start?" Marcus had crossed his arms, clearly getting more and more irritated by the second.

"Okay... My name isn't really Logan."

If Marcus was shocked by that piece of information, I couldn't tell. His expression remained neutral as he stared at me. While I wasn't scared of him in any way, his intense focus was now making me squirm a little.

"That's actually my boss's name. Well, probably my former boss now, but it's not me."

"I know."

"You see, last Friday when I— Wait, you *know*?"

"Yes. I know. I knew the second that *Cole* stepped into the conference room with us. I assume that was Logan?"

I opened my mouth about to answer or ask why he hadn't given me up then and there. But before I could get the words out, Marcus was already speaking again.

"I don't appreciate being lied to or being made a fool of. You've managed to achieve both of those things within a week of knowing me."

"I didn't mean to—"

"I'm not finished yet."

I clamped my mouth shut as Marcus sat forward and clasped his hands on the desk.

"Last Friday was a one-off. Something I never do, and clearly shouldn't have this time."

I worried my bottom lip with my teeth, and Marcus's eyes dropped to the move. It was the first time he'd showed any interest in me beyond irritation, and it sparked a glimmer of hope deep down inside—like, waaaay deep down.

"But you enjoyed it. Right?"

Marcus's cool eyes roved back up to my face, and while the intensity in his stare would've made the most steely-nerved cower, I found myself captivated by the promise of his wrath.

"I did."

See? I knew it. I just needed to appeal to the side I'd discovered last week. I'd done it once before—how hard could it be to get him back there?

"That doesn't negate the fact that due to your lie, I still don't know *whom* I enjoyed myself with. Does it?"

Oh... Yeah, it might help if I told him that.

"My name's Gabriel. Gabriel Romero. I usually go by Gabe."

Marcus sat forward in his seat, and my breath caught as his eyes did another slow, leisurely sweep of me. I was almost convinced all was forgiven when a drilling sound echoed throughout out the room.

I whirled around in my seat to see where it was coming from, then turned back to face Marcus, who nodded.

"Yes. That's security—just in case you were wondering. They're removing the door handle that you locked so they can come in here and escort you out of the building."

My eyes widened. "Escort me *out*? But... I—"

"That's what tends to happen when a strange man bursts into my office and then locks himself in here."

"Can't you... I don't know..." I sputtered. "Call them off or something?"

Marcus stood and loomed over me from behind his desk.

"I could." He paused as the door was thrown open and two hulking men rushed into the room. "But that would be much less enjoyable for me."

His wolfish smirk was as shocking as it was sexy. But before I could even begin to dissect my screwed-up reaction to it, two men flanked me and hooked an arm under each of my elbows.

"I can walk on my own," I snapped, and glared at the one to my left.

Completely ignoring me, he looked to Marcus. "Are you okay, Mr. St. James? Are you injured in any way?"

Injured? He wasn't right now, but give me two seconds and I was sure I could locate something to throw at his head.

"No, I'm fine thank you, Everett." Marcus's eyes then cut to mine. "If you could just escort Mr....*Romero* here out of the building, I think that will deter him from coming back in the future."

My mouth fell open, and I couldn't help but make a horrified sound. Was he kidding right now? Was he really going to throw me out? But when the two guards began tugging me around the chair and back toward the door, I began to struggle.

"Marcus? Come on."

He said nothing as they continued to haul me toward the door, merely arched one of his brows over his arctic-blue eyes.

When the three of us reached the door and I was just about to be pulled through it, I heard him say, "On your way out, could you let Carmen know to call up a locksmith? I think it's time I added some reinforcements to prevent future issues."

"Of course, sir."

I narrowed my eyes as Marcus's glinted under the lights. Icy bastard was enjoying this. But if he thought this was the last he'd see of me, he had another thing coming.

Logan had been very clear with me earlier: get Marcus to forgive me or don't bother coming back—and since I kind of liked eating, it looked like my ability to stoop low was about to be tested.

CHAPTER 11

MARCUS

IT WAS COMING up to that time of the day when I made myself shut down and finally head home. The sun had just about disappeared and given way to night, and as I shut off my computer, grabbed up my briefcase, and made my way across my office to the door, I looked at the shiny new handle and shook my head.

It wasn't often that I was blindsided by life, but I had to admit that Logan—*Gabe*—had caught me completely off guard, *twice* now. The first time with his devastatingly good looks, and the second time by the bold audacity he seemed to run around life with.

It had been that boldness that was the icing on the cake the night we met. Yes, I'd been attracted, but that wouldn't have been enough to make me leave a work function to get him somewhere alone.

That had been due to the charming yet arrogant way he chased me down. He'd shown no hesitation, no reluctance to go after what he wanted, and that night, he'd definitely gotten it.

But that was where it would end. I didn't have the time or the inclination to deal with someone who used anything to get ahead, even a lie. That wasn't for me, and I didn't have time to deal with *anyone*, period.

What I'd said was true the night I met Gabe: work was my partner in life. It was demanding, frustrating, but extremely rewarding when everything went right, and at this stage, I wasn't prepared to push that aside for anything other than sheer perfection.

I made my way down the hall and gave a clipped nod to Carmen on my way out. It didn't matter what time I left; she never did until I was gone for the evening. I felt guilty about that at times, but she'd never expressed the desire for it to be any other way, so I left it as it was.

I rode the elevator down alone and was grateful not to have to participate in frivolous small talk with anyone. When I reached the bottom, I made a beeline for the doors.

Carmen would've called ahead for my car, and as I stepped out onto the sidewalk, I was brought up short by Gabe leaning against a *No Parking* sign.

With his hands shoved in his pockets and his legs crossed at the ankles, he looked cool and casual, which seemed to be his way. But when he looked up and spotted me, I noticed the fatigue in his eyes.

What was he doing out here? It was nearly six in the evening. Had he been waiting here all day?

I marched over to him, and as he shoved off the pole and

straightened to his full height, I asked, "What are you still doing here?"

Several passersby looked our way. But when they caught sight of my *there's nothing to see here* expression, they kept right on going.

Gabe ran a hand through his thick, windswept hair, brushing it back from his face. Then he shrugged, looking far too sexy for his own good.

"I've been waiting for you."

"It's nearly *six* o'clock."

Gabe nodded. "I'm aware."

"And you've been waiting out here since..." I looked at my watch, trying to work out how long it had been since—

"Eleven forty-five, when you threw me out."

"Are you insane?"

Gabe pondered that for a second, then he shook his head. "No, not insane. Not crazy, either. I am, however, in need of a job, and my boss told me not to come back unless I made things right with you. After the whole throwing-me-out-of-your-office deal, I figured we weren't quite there yet."

I pressed my fingers to my forehead. "And you think *this* is the right way to get there?"

"Well, it was kind of the only thing I could think of, so I just went with it."

"You seem to do that a lot."

"What?"

"Go with the first thing that enters your mind."

Gabe angled his chin up. "I didn't hear you complaining."

No, he most certainly hadn't. I'd been too captivated by him that night to complain, just as I found myself now.

"And what exactly is your plan now?" I asked. "Wait out here until morning?"

"No. I was hoping you'd let me talk to you and explain—"

I held up a hand. "I don't mean to sound…"

"Cold?"

I ground my molars together, ignoring that. "But I don't want an explanation. Nothing you have to say will change the fact that you lied about who you were and what you did for a living. It's done, it's over with, and maybe it'll teach you a lesson somewhere down the track."

Just as I finished talking, Franklin—my driver—pulled up to the curb in the black Cadillac Escalade the company provided. I opened the door and climbed inside, and just as I went to shut it, Gabe scooted in behind me.

"What the hell do you think you're doing?"

I didn't have time to wait for an answer, unless I wanted to end up with a lap full of Gabe. So I shifted to the other side of the vehicle and watched in stunned silence as he shut the door behind him.

This guy either had no fear or no brains; I couldn't work out which.

"Get out of my car."

Gabe reached for his seatbelt, fastened it, then shook his head. "No."

"No?"

"Yeah, no. I need you to listen to me, and this seems like the best way for that to happen."

"This is not the best way. In fact, the only thing this is best for is getting yourself arrested."

Gabe leaned back against the side of the door and looked me over. "See, I think you're lying."

"Mr. St. James? Do we have a problem?"

We didn't, but *I* most certainly did. One that came in a five-eleven frame with bronze skin, and messy sex hair that made me think of how it would look after a night in my bed.

"Everything is fine, Franklin. We can go."

Gabe's eyes widened as though he was shocked that I hadn't tossed him out of the car. I couldn't blame him. The thought had crossed my mind. But something about the fact that he'd waited nearly six hours outside made even my jaded heart give pause.

As Franklin merged with the rush-hour traffic, I looked over to see Gabe grinning.

"See, I knew you were lying. You aren't going to call the cops on me."

"Keep it up and you'll see just how wrong you are."

"Mhmm." Gabe settled into the leather seat. "Then why am I still sitting here?"

"Because it somehow seems wrong to throw you out of a moving car."

"Oh, gotcha, you only do it out of stationary buildings."

My lips twitched despite myself. "You have a smart mouth."

"You would know."

I eyed him for a couple of seconds. "You mentioned your boss wants you to fix what you did? How is irritating me supposed to achieve that, do you think?"

"Well..." Gabe worried his lower lip with his teeth, and I was reminded of how soft and pliable that mouth had felt under mine. "I hadn't gotten that far yet, but I'm sure it had something to do with my ever-present charm."

"You are definitely ever-present."

"That's not what I meant."

"And yet it's still true. So what is it you are hoping to get out of this? A pat on the head from me? An 'it's okay, we're all fine now'? Or do I need to write you a note for you to take back to your boss?"

Gabe pondered that for a moment. "Actually, I'm not sure. Maybe I should call him?"

"Don't you think that all of this is slightly undignified?"

"As opposed to earlier this morning, when I had to tell my boss I pretended to be him and then got physically removed from a building by two men? No, actually, this feels like the perfect end to this day. The only way it would be more fitting is if you made me grovel on my knees. Then I'd say it went down pretty much the way I expected it to."

I wondered how long it would take for him to realize what he had just—

"Shit."

—said.

"I didn't mean that the way it sounded."

"No?"

"*No.*" Gabe shook his head. "Despite what you think of me, I don't sleep with men who don't like me."

"Only men who don't know your name."

He clicked his teeth shut at the low blow I'd just delivered, and while it was an accurate enough statement, I felt like an asshole for having said it. Gabe turned away and looked out the window, and I wondered if he'd finally given up.

"So, how about this... I'll do whatever you want for the next week straight. No questions asked."

Apparently not. "*Whatever* I want? That's a very broad playing field."

"I don't mean sex. Well, maybe— No, I don't mean sex. I mean, of course I'd love to pay off my debt that way, but we're talking about my job here. I'm trying to act professional."

"Professional? And what exactly is professional about your jumping in the back of my car and refusing to get out?"

"Okay, well, I'm trying to act professional from now *on.*"

"Right, and you think you can abide by those terms?"

"Of course I can. I won't use my body to get my job back."

I eyed him for a beat and then gave a clipped nod. "Okay."

He opened his mouth, clearly ready to argue some more, but when he realized I'd just agreed, he frowned. "Good."

"Good, I'm glad that's settled. Now, back to what you *are* going to do to get your job back."

I could see the wheels turning behind his eyes.

"Well, you seem like a pretty important guy who probably needs a million things done. So when I'm not at work, I'll...be at your beck and call. Anything you need or want, something picked up, dinner delivered, your car serviced... I'll do it."

"What if I want dinner at three in the morning?"

"Then I'll bring you dinner at three in the morning. In exchange, you promise not to do anything to jeopardize Mitchell & Madison's chances of landing Tennant's account."

Hmm, now this could be interesting.

Franklin pulled up to the curb outside my home. As I looked to my stowaway, I saw he was leaning forward and peering around me out the window with a slack-jawed expression.

"*That's* where you live?"

I glanced out the window at the home that took up a full corner block of the city, and then turned back to Gabe. "Yes."

A frown formed between his brows. "Isn't that like a museum or something?"

I could understand why he thought that. My place was a well-known landmark in the city. "No. It's my home. It's on the national register as a historical landmark, but it is very much a private residence."

"Holy shit, and Lake Michigan is right there."

I nodded, but was far more interested in discussing the terms he'd brought up a minute ago. "Back to this little deal you're proposing."

Gabe dragged his gaze away from the window and focused on me. "Yes?"

"You said one week?"

A wide grin curved those lying lips. "One week."

"Give me your phone."

His eyes widened a fraction, but then he shoved his hips up to fish around for his cell, and I couldn't stop my eyes from falling to the tight fit of his pants. That was a mistake, because immediately I thought of the sound he'd made when I pulled a similar pair off him last week.

"Here you go."

He held his phone out to me and then lowered his eyes to my mouth. It seemed I wasn't the only one remembering that night.

I took the cell, quickly added my number, and handed it back to him. He looked at the digits and smiled again.

"Text me," I said before he shut it off.

Gabe began to type, and the next thing I knew, a text with his number appeared on my phone.

Good evening, Mr. St. James. How can I be of service to you tonight?

Before I gave in and suggested all the ways I'd like him to service me, I reached for my briefcase and shoved open my door. When Gabe did the same, I looked over at him. "What are you doing?"

He gestured outside. "I was going to go and call an Uber."

Even I wasn't that heartless. While Gabe might've

brought his current predicament on himself, I wasn't about to make him go and catch an Uber home.

"Franklin? Will you please take Mr. Romero wherever it is he needs to go?"

"Of course, Mr. St. James."

When I looked back to Gabe, he mouthed, *So fancy.*

I shook my head and reached for the door again. "You'll be hearing from me."

I slammed the door shut before he could reply. I needed a drink and I needed it now, but as I made my way to the front door, I couldn't help but take one final look at the SUV.

So he wanted to work off his debt, did he? Well, I was sure I could come up with something suitable to make him grovel. Poor Gabe—he had no idea what he'd just agreed to, but he would soon enough.

CHAPTER 12

GABE

MARCUS GAVE ME his number, his actual, real, honest-to-God phone number, and as Franklin pulled away from the incredible home he'd just dropped Marcus at, I looked at the digits staring back at me and couldn't help but grin.

I'd made one hell of a gamble in waiting for him today. When he tossed me out this morning, I'd thought about going back to Mitchell & Madison defeated. But I also knew the only thing waiting for me if I did that would be a cardboard box and Logan directing me to the nearest exit.

So I'd taken a chance. I'd waited for Marcus for *hours*. Oh, I'd taken the occasional break to grab a coffee and some lunch, but I made sure my ass was in a seat where I could watch the entrance to his building. I'd been convinced that all I needed was five minutes—ten max—of his time to persuade him that he should forgive me, and lo and behold, I was right.

Now to tell Logan. I scrolled through my contacts until I came to his number and hit call. Then I waited and waited and waited. I frowned and pulled the phone from my ear to look at the screen, and yep, I'd definitely called the right number. That was when it connected.

"Hello?" Logan shouted over the far-off sound of voices and thumping music, and I had to strain to hear him.

"Logan? It's Gabe."

There was the distinct sound of someone moving. "Who?"

Oh, great. He'd probably already fired me and blocked me from his mind.

"Gabe! Your—"

"Bitch? Oh, yeah, I can hear you now. Sorry, the bar's a little loud tonight."

That made sense—he was at his husband's place, The Popped Cherry. I'd definitely have to check that out at some stage.

"So, tell me, Gabe. Do I still have a PA, or am I back to the horrid task of interviewing?"

I sure hope not. "You still have a PA. I spoke to Mr. St. James."

"And?"

"And we cleared up our little...misunderstanding."

"Should I even ask?"

I stared out at the lights of the passing cars. "Probably not. Just know it's fixed and it won't affect the deal, or you, in any way."

There was no response, only a faint, thumping beat. "Logan?"

"I'm here. I was just letting you sweat it out." I could almost see his cunning grin. "Okay, let's leave it at that and never talk about this again. Yes?"

God yes.

"I'll see you tomorrow, Gabe."

"See you then."

When Logan ended the call, I let out a relieved sigh and closed my eyes. That'd been close, but it seemed I would live to see another day.

As I settled in for the rest of the trip home, it occurred to me that I was now indebted to not one, but *two* men in my life. How the hell had that happened? Oh, that's right: I'd tried to swim with the big fish—or more like *whales*.

Ryan had warned me. I was itty-bitty, and Marcus was out of my league. Boy had he been right. The guy practically had a person for anything and everything he needed, and tonight he'd added one more.

When Franklin pulled up outside my apartment building, I said my thank-yous and waved goodbye, then headed inside. I was dying to get out of this suit, shower, and lie down for the next twelve hours. My feet were killing me after waiting on the sidewalk all day, and all I wanted was to be horizontal.

After a quick ride up to the tenth floor, I got out and headed down to mine and Ryan's apartment. It was to the left and all the way down the other end of the hall. I didn't usually mind that, since it meant we only had neighbors on the one side. But tonight, it felt like a million miles away.

I unlocked the door and practically fell inside, and lucky for me, my room was directly off the front entrance. I spotted Ryan on the couch watching TV and threw him a wave, but my bed beckoned, and honestly, I wasn't sure I'd make it to the shower.

As I fell facedown into my mattress, I heard Ryan open the door behind me and barely smothered a groan in the pillow.

"I know you aren't used to this whole nine-to-five gig yet, but you look close to paralytic."

I *felt* close to paralytic. But somehow, I managed to roll myself over. "It's been a *long* day." Understatement of the century.

"Really?" Ryan grimaced, thinking I meant a long day at my new job. "Want to talk about it?"

I did, but I had no idea where to even start. "Maybe later?"

"Sure, maybe after you've slept."

Sleep...that sounded like heaven right about now.

"Before you zone out, though, want to know what happened at *my* job today?" Ryan waggled his eyebrows, and my ears immediately pricked up. "Apparently, some lunatic burst into Marcus's office and locked himself in there. Then—wait for it—*Marcus* had the guy thrown out. As in physically picked up and thrown out of the building. Can you believe that shit?"

Yeah, I actually could.

"That guy." Ryan shook his head. "I told you, he's made of *ice*. I mean, you know, you met him that night, and even you couldn't get him to crack. Now *that's* saying something."

Sooo, I hadn't been exactly honest about what happened the night of Ryan's office party. But I hadn't been sure how he'd react to my hookup with his boss's boss and decided to keep it to myself, since I never planned to see Marcus again. Since that ship had clearly sailed, it seemed now was as good as time as any to confess my sins.

"About that," I said.

"About what?"

"The, um, night of the work party."

"Yeah? What about it?"

I scrubbed a hand over my face and then pushed it back through my hair. "I didn't exactly leave when I said I did."

"What do you mean?" Ryan frowned. "You said you weren't feeling good that night."

"Right, uh, I lied."

Ryan eyed me and sat down on the bed. "You *lied*? So what really happened?"

I looked at him and winced. "I hooked up with Marcus."

Ryan shoved me so hard in the arm that I fell back on my bed. "You did *not*."

"I did." I sat up and rubbed the spot he'd just whacked.

"How? I mean...where? Actually, don't answer that, I don't want to know, but—*Marcus*? Really?"

"Yeah."

"Oh my God. That face of yours really *does* get you whoever you want, doesn't it?"

I shoved *him* this time. "Thanks a lot. I do have a personality, you know."

"I know, but let's be real. The first thing everyone sees is this." Ryan waved a hand in front of my face. "The personality is second. Although I can't imagine the Almighty crumbling just because of the way someone looks. You must have made one hell of a first impression."

Yeah, as someone else.

"So," Ryan said. "How did that all end? Are you two seeing each other again?"

I couldn't help but laugh. Then I laughed and laughed some more, and I was so tired it sounded almost delirious.

"Gabe?"

"Sorry." I tried to rein in my hilarity, but when I thought over the day's events, it got the better of me all over again. When I finally got myself under some kind of control, I said, "It was me."

Ryan frowned, clearly confused, and I couldn't blame him.

"The crazed lunatic in his office today? That was me."

Ryan's eyes widened until they looked as though they might pop out of their sockets. "Are you kidding right now?"

I shook my head.

"*Gabe!* Are you insane? That's where I work."

"I know," I said as I got to my aching feet and cursed.

"Wait a minute. *Wait* a minute. This doesn't make any sense. What am I missing here? You two hooked up a week ago, and today when you went to see him, he threw you *out?*"

I quickly looked away from him and shrugged out of my jacket.

"Okay, what did you do?"

I opened my closet and pulled out a hanger. "What makes you think I did something?"

Ryan got to his feet and came over to me. "I know you—that's what makes me think that. And when you saw Marcus, you were laser-focused on getting him. How'd you pull it off?"

I gnawed on my lower lip and let out a sigh. Then I told him about the whole name debacle, the mix-up at Mitchell & Madison, and Logan's ultimatum about fixing things or not coming back. By the time I got near the end, where I'd thrown myself across the back seat of Marcus's car, Ryan looked close to apoplectic.

"Then what happened?"

"We made a deal. For the next week, when I'm not at my real job, I'm basically *his* off-the-clock personal assistant."

"Marcus's?"

"Yeah."

Ryan crossed his arms and eyed me. "So basically, you'll work all day and then come home and do whatever he wants when you're free?"

"Yeah. I guess."

"So you're going to take a whole week off from practice... for him? Is that really smart?"

No, but what else was I going to do? Yes, I would have to put a few things on hold to do this, but it was just a week.

For the first time in months, I was allowing myself a moment to forget everything I now had to work doubly hard for. It would all still be there after. But Marcus might not be. "You do realize I'm not in school anymore, right?"

"Yes, but you're the one who told me that you needed to practice to keep your hands in shape and your ear sharp."

"I know," I said a little more forcefully than I intended. "But a few days off is not going make a difference, then I'll get right back to it."

"Okay, you know best. Just be careful." Ryan walked to the door, shaking his head.

"Why? I'm just going to be running some errands here and there."

"I mean, okay. It's just—" He stopped and looked at me kicking off my shoes, awake enough now to have a quick shower before bed.

"What? Do you think he's still going to mess with the deal for Logan?"

"No. I think he's going to mess with *you*. I'm not sure it's worth it."

I rolled my eyes and made my way over to Ryan. "I'll be fine. It's just a week."

He stepped out of my way and shrugged. "Okay. But don't say I didn't warn you."

As I crossed the living room toward the bathroom, I looked back at him. "Remember, you're the one who said I couldn't get him to look twice at me."

"And look how well that worked out."

"Exactly—he did a whole lot more than look."

"And here you are now, his puppet for a week."

Oh yeah...

"Just be careful. I don't want you to get hurt. Marcus is a rock; he doesn't budge. He got his reputation for a reason. He's used to reigning supreme. Don't think you can outplay him."

I waved him off, but as I shut the bathroom door, I pulled up Marcus's number, opened the contact, and quickly typed in something that would remind me exactly who I was dealing with whenever he called. Then I hit save and turned on the shower, ready to wash today's humiliation down the drain so I was ready for whatever tomorrow would bring.

CHAPTER 13

MARCUS

I WAS A good sleeper for the most part. A workaholic by nature, when I finally did switch off, I had no problem winding down and turning the lights out for the handful of hours my body needed, so I could recharge and get back to it all again the next day.

But tonight my brain wasn't having a bar of it. It was working overtime trying to figure out whose head it was trapped inside, because the impulsive moron who'd struck a deal with a man who'd lied his way into my pants and then my office couldn't possibly be me.

Except it was, and every time Gabriel Romero walked into my life, I seemed to lose all sense of reason and found myself doing the exact opposite to what I usually would. Like this evening in my car. I should've demanded he get out. Hell, I should've had Franklin *drag* him out. Instead, I'd found myself wanting to know whatever new scheme he was dreaming up to stay in my company, and it appeared Gabe had many.

He was fast-thinking, confident, and incredibly charming. So not only was I trying to ignore a face that made thinking a challenge, I was fighting the desire to keep him around for pure enjoyment—and I could think of many ways to enjoy him.

I snatched up the crystal carafe that sat on the bottom shelf of my bookcase and poured myself a finger of scotch before heading over to the window. It was early Friday morning, and as I swirled the alcohol around in my glass, the color reminded me of Gabe's eyes and the way they seemed to glow when he was aroused.

This wasn't the first time I'd revisited the night we met. But it was the first time I had his real name.

Gabriel... Gabe...

It suited him, and when I thought of the way he'd looked with his back up against the wall of Studio A and my hand down his pants, my cock hardened.

That was going to be a problem, one I'd almost given in to twice today. Once in my office and again in the back of my company car. Gabe got close and I had a difficult time keeping my hands to myself. It was clear he was trouble, and if I was smart, I'd keep him exactly where I'd put him—as far away from me as possible. That was the main reason I'd let Everett and Tom throw him out earlier. I'd been about ten seconds away from marching around the desk and demanding that he *beg* for my forgiveness, and that wouldn't have helped anything.

I shook my head and downed the scotch in one quick swallow, enjoying the smooth, rich flavor as it made a fiery path down my throat. Then I slid the glass onto my desk and flicked the lamp off.

I made my way through the dark halls of the house to the winding staircase that led to the bedrooms on the second floor. When I reached mine, I headed straight inside and climbed into bed, hoping the alcohol would take the edge off and let me fall asleep.

About to switch my phone to vibrate—I always left the notifications on in case the world went to shit at one a.m. and I needed to be reached—I realized it was well *past* one now, and was actually creeping up to three.

I smiled and shifted to my side, thinking what better time to make sure my new errand boy was indeed at my beck and call whenever I desired.

I shifted to my side, propped myself up on my elbow, and typed: **Good morning, Gabe, are you awake?**

It was possible I'd get no response—after all, it was nearly three. But when dots appeared on my screen, indicating Gabe was responding, so did my body, with the sudden spike in my heart rate.

Good morning? This isn't morning, there's actually no greeting for what this is because no one should be up.

Tell that to my cock, I thought as I stared down at the tented sheet resting across my lap. It had reacted as though Gabe had stepped into the room with me, and *that* was the problem. Yet here I was, eagerly responding.

I don't care about anyone else. I'm awake, and if I'm not mistaken, you signed on the be at MY beck and call, didn't you?

Three dots...pause...three dots...pause.

He was clearly trying to decide on what to type next, but then my phone began to ring and Gabe's name appeared on the screen.

The smart thing to do would be to hit *decline* and let it go straight to voicemail. But from the moment Gabe walked into my life, the "smart thing" had seemed like the least desirable option.

Instead, I slid down beneath my sheets and hit *accept*.

"You called, Mr. St. James?"

My lips twitched. Even at three in the morning, Gabe was a smartass. "Something I'm quickly regretting."

He laughed, and his good nature, even as I disturbed his sleep, said a lot about the man that pleased me, despite myself.

"You know, for someone who was so upset that I lied about my name, you really should practice what you preach."

"Excuse me?"

"You should tell the truth."

"I am telling the truth."

Gabe tsked. "See, you're lying again. You don't regret answering the phone. The only thing you regret is that I'm not lying in your bed beside you, *which*, by the way, is your own fault."

"My fault? You made the deal not to use your body to rectify a situation that you created."

"Only after my job was threatened. If you hadn't stormed out of Mitchell & Madison, we could've worked this out and I could've been in your bed. Therefore, this is your fault."

It would've been outrageous had it not been true. To not get caught up in another lie, however, I decided to redirect this conversation.

"And is that why you called me? Because you couldn't fit all of that in a text?"

"No... I don't actually know why I called."

I did. It was for the exact same reason I'd yet to hang up. It appeared that now that we knew how to get into contact with one another, we were having trouble staying away.

"Gabe?"

I heard the rustle of sheets and tried not to picture what he might or might not wear to bed. "Yeah?"

"You should get some sleep."

"Well, I was, until some crazy man with my number texted me."

"Uh huh." I looked at the clock on my nightstand. "I'll see you in a couple of hours."

"A couple of *hours*?"

That woke him up.

"Yes. I just remembered I forgot to pick up some coffee for tomorrow, so I expect you on my doorstep at five o'clock. Have a grande Blonde Roast and an everything bagel with you from the Starbucks on State and Delaware, and be sure to get the morning paper from them. Did you get all that?"

I could hear him sputtering a little, which made me smile.

"If you didn't, just tell them Marcus sent you. Sleep well, Gabe. I have a feeling you're going to need it."

CHAPTER 14
GABE

FOUR FORTY-FIVE A.M. and I was pulling open the front door to Starbucks with a yawn. I'd barely gotten any sleep after Marcus had given me the God-awful task of getting up before the sun rose. But I wasn't going to be defeated. I was in this for the long haul. I'd made a deal and I intended to keep my side of it, even if by the end of the week I fell into a coma.

I moved into line behind the other poor souls who were up this early and covered a second yawn. This just wasn't normal; the only reason anyone should be up this early was if they had a hot body beside them wanting a morning workout.

As person after person placed their order and shuffled off to the side to wait, my phone began to vibrate in my pocket. There was only one person I knew who would call me at this hour, and despite my current lack of cheer, I hit *accept* and brought the phone to my ear.

"I'm sorry, I can't talk right now. I'm asleep in line at Starbucks."

Marcus's deep chuckle was filled with vengeful pleasure, and still it managed to send a frisson of electricity through me.

"That's good to know. I was calling to make sure you hadn't slept through your alarm."

"More like calling to make sure you weren't about to miss your morning coffee."

"That too. But more so on whether I needed to send someone in your place."

I scoffed and moved up the line. "Must be nice to have so many people to do your bidding."

"They're paid well to do so, so I'm sure they don't mind. *You*, on the other hand, I have to keep a careful eye on."

Jesus. Something about the way he said that made every nerve ending in my body come alive, as I imagined him stretched out in his bed with his eyes locked on me.

"Gabe?"

I quickly shoved aside that image and noticed I was up next. "I'm here, but I have to go. I have an order to place for a workaholic who needs to learn to sleep longer."

"Very well. I'll see you soon."

That sounded more like a threat than a goodbye, and my body was all about it, my dick throbbing at the idea of seeing him again—and soon. When I reached the counter, I placed Marcus's order exactly as instructed and made sure to add who it was for. The woman smiled then reached under the counter for a paper and handed it to me.

"We always make sure to keep Mr. St. James a copy for when he stops in."

Of course they did. "Thank you."

"You're welcome. Your coffees will be ready in a minute."

"Coffees? I only ordered the one and a bagel."

She smiled and scribbled a name on the cup she was holding. "Oh, I know. But Mr. St. James called a little earlier and had us take down his order. He said to just make those instead and give them to you."

Was he kidding right now? What, he didn't think I'd remember *two* coffee orders? Why'd he even bother sending me in the first place? Oh, that's right, because he was punishing me.

I nodded to the woman and tried for a smile. After all, this wasn't her fault. Then I moved to the side to wait and called an Uber. It didn't take long for the coffees to arrive— Marcus's roast and some icy concoction I assumed was for an employee of his—and after she called me up and I got everything balanced and in hand, I made my way out to the curb and stopped dead in my tracks.

"Franklin?"

"Good Morning, Mr. Romero."

Good Lord, does this man ever sleep?

"Uh, hi." Then I spotted the Escalade and narrowed my eyes. "Is he in there?"

There was no need for me to say his name. Franklin knew exactly who I meant.

"No, sir, I'm here to pick you up."

As my sleep-addled brain tried to make sense of that, my phone lit up and I realized my Uber was waiting for me. There was nothing I would've enjoyed more than telling Franklin *thanks but no thanks*, just to stick it to Marcus. But it would save me money, and that was a factor right now.

I balanced the coffees, bagel, and paper in one hand, pulled my phone out with the other, and cancelled the ride. Then I turned back to Franklin.

"Okay, let's go."

I climbed inside the SUV and was extra careful not to spill anything on the pristine interior, then I settled in for the short ride back to Marcus's place. It was still dark outside, and when Franklin pulled up at the front gate, I looked up at the towering structure before me in awe. It really was like looking into the past.

"Sir? Mr. St. James is waiting for you."

"Oh, sorry. Thanks for the ride."

"Of course."

I pushed open the door and somehow managed to climb out even with my hands full, and then made my way to the steps, where I pushed the doorbell.

Not a second later, it was pulled open and I was shocked to see Marcus standing on the other side. Not shocked because he was there but shocked that *he'd* opened the door. I'd expected him to have a butler.

He had his phone to his ear but waved me inside. He closed the door as I crossed the threshold, and I turned to see him pacing to one side of the entryway, which gave me a good opportunity to look him over.

Half-dressed for work, Marcus was in a pair of pressed pants that molded to an ass I'd had my hands all over. He wore a fitted white shirt that was tucked in at his waist, and minus his jacket, I was able to see for the first time the true outline of his powerful frame.

I'd known he was built, especially after he pinned me against the studio wall, but seeing his wide shoulders, trim waist, and long legs all neatly packaged, with nothing hindering my view, was a completely different experience to imagining it.

"I understand that, Glenn," Marcus said in a tone that could cut through steel. "But there's no space for his opinion when he's delivering a factual news story. Brian knows better, and was bullshitting because he didn't agree with what he was reporting on. Tell him that I expect to see his ass in my office at three this afternoon—sharp."

Shit. I wasn't sure who Glenn was, or whom he had the pleasant task of telling that Marcus wanted to see them. But speaking from experience, that office didn't bode well for those who entered it.

Not wanting to incur the wrath of an irritated Marcus, I turned away to give him some privacy and got my first real look at the inside of his house. I'd known from the outside that the interior would be something spectacular, but the elegant marble floors, paired with the rich wooden paneling, were truly breathtaking. So much so that I didn't actually want to step off the entryway rug.

Marcus had said the place was registered as a historic landmark, so I'd looked it up before I fell asleep last night.

I'd found out that it had been built in the nineteenth century, and somewhere in the back of my head I'd associated that with an old, outdated home inside.

How wrong was I? His place was gorgeous, and so far, all I could see was the front entrance.

"I see you found Franklin."

I turned to see Marcus directly behind me, and schooled my features to neutral as I held out the coffee tray.

"Actually, he found me. I thought you wanted *me* to bring you your coffee this morning."

"I did." Marcus took the large cup from the tray, and then reached for the newspaper tucked under my arm. "I wanted Franklin to bring me you."

I opened my mouth to tell him I would've gotten here on my own, but Marcus gestured to the other coffee.

"That's yours. I believe I owed you a drink."

At the reminder of our night together, my heart began to thump a little harder. "How did you know I like coffee?"

"I didn't. But I figured it's early, and you were up late, and if I remember correctly, you like things a little...salty. Linda, at Starbucks, recommended that."

I looked down to the icy concoction still in the tray, then dragged my finger through the whipped topping and looked up at him. "Good guess. I like salty *and* creamy."

Marcus arched a brow but otherwise ignored the remark. "I just need to get my jacket and we'll be on our way."

As he walked away from me, I called out, "What? No personal tour this time?"

Marcus paused, but even with the distance separating us there was no missing the heat now simmering.

"Not this time, no."

It was on the tip of my tongue to say, *But maybe* next *time?* Then I remembered that I was the one who'd told him I wouldn't use my body as payment on this deal and wanted to slap myself.

Instead, I swiped my finger through the cream again and sucked it into my mouth, and took great delight when Marcus watched. Two could play at this little game. He wanted to torture me by making me do his bidding over the next week? Then I would do my very best to torture him into giving in and doing *my* bidding when this was all over.

Now *that* was a deal that I could get on board with.

CHAPTER 15

MARCUS

ALK AWAY. TURN around and walk away from him.

I didn't know how many times I must've repeated that to myself as I tore my eyes away from Gabe, who was standing in my front entrance sucking whipped cream off his finger. But minutes later I was still saying it as I entered my office and put my jacket on, because my God, what a picture he made.

It didn't matter where he was: a party, an office, a sidewalk, or my foyer at five in the morning. Gabe was tempting in any and all situations, it seemed, and I had a hell of a difficult time keeping an air of indifference around him. Something I never usually had an issue with.

Giving myself an extra minute or two to squash the arousal he stirred in me, I took the time to send a quick email to Carmen about fitting in a meeting this afternoon with Brian Evans—the fool—and then straightened my tie.

You'd think having an imbecile for one of my afternoon anchors would be enough to distract me from wanting to rip Gabe's clothes off. But it seemed my libido had reverted to that of a horny teenager. The second he dipped his finger in that creamy drink and sucked it clean, my cock had decided it wanted to be next, which was a bad idea for so many reasons.

Gabe had to be at least ten years my junior, which was reason enough to cut this off immediately. But he was making me feel things I hadn't felt in years, and I still wasn't sure what I wanted to do about that.

I stepped out of my office and saw him with his back to me as he looked at his surroundings, and as I made my way down the hall, I let my eyes travel the length of his suit. It fit him well enough, but the jacket was about half a size too big for him and the pants scrunched around his ankles, and I got the distinct impression this wasn't his usual attire, since he'd clearly not had them altered yet.

When he heard my approach, Gabe turned and pulled his drink straw free of his lips.

"This is delicious."

I looked at his half-finished drink. "So I see."

"Have you ever tried it?"

"I don't drink those kinds of drinks."

Gabe smirked, and those cheeky dimples flirted with me. "What, delicious ones?"

"The iced, sugary-sweet coffee ones. Give me straight black, hard-hitting caffeine any day."

Gabe took another sip and then waggled his brows at

me. "I bet you'd like it if you tried it. Come on, have a sip," he said, and held the drink out to me.

I took a step forward and reached out as though I was about to take it from him. But at the last second I wrapped my fingers around his wrist and tugged him in until his shoes bumped up against mine.

He craned his head back and took in a deep breath. I glanced at his drink and then brought my eyes back to his. When he swallowed, I knew he could see the desire I could no longer hide swirling in my eyes.

"There's only thing I want to suck in this house right now, and I promise you it's not that straw. But since you made that asinine rule that your body couldn't be part of our little bargain, I suggest you stop teasing me and get your ass out my front door and back in the car."

Gabe licked at his lower lip as his gaze roved down to my mouth, and my cock hardened.

He triumphantly grinned and then took a step back, grabbed the brown paper bag he'd placed on the entryway table, and held it out to me.

"Your bagel, Mr. St. James."

I took it from him and picked up my briefcase in my other hand. I pulled open the door, and as Gabe passed by me he said, "Is there anything in your life that isn't exactly where it's supposed to be?"

"You. But I'm making an exception."

He nodded and then continued outside and down the stairs. When he reached the curb, he waved.

"Good morning again, Franklin."

My dour, straight-faced driver's lips twitched as he gave a curt nod. "Mr. Romero."

I watched the exchange with fascination as Gabe disappeared inside the car. When I approached, Franklin reached for my briefcase.

"Good morning, Mr. St. James."

"Morning, Franklin."

"Straight to the office this morning, sir?"

"Yes, thank you."

"Of course." He held the door open and shut it behind me. I settled in and, once my belt was fastened, looked over to find Gabe watching me with a grin.

"And what dare I ask is so amusing?"

"You. You're always so serious, even when you say good morning. Wait, sorry, you didn't say *good*."

"Maybe I'm not having a good morning."

Gabe pulled a face that said he seriously doubted that. "Okay, you keep telling yourself that."

Arrogant. I pulled my phone out and was about to do my second scroll through of the morning news when Gabe reached over and took it from my hands.

"What do you think you're doing? Give that back."

"I don't think so." Gabe tucked the phone under his thigh. "If I have to sit in this car with you at five in the morning while you get *driven* to work, then the least you can do is have a conversation with me."

"That wasn't part of the deal."

"Too bad. If I have to be up this early *and* catch an Uber to my real job later, then you can entertain me."

"Franklin will take you to work."

"Franklin needs to eat."

"He eats."

"Really? When does he sleep?"

I sighed and rubbed at my beard. Gabe wanted to have a conversation, did he? Okay, I could work with that—there were definitely things I was curious about. The fact I was allowing him to hold my phone ransom was a testament to the fact that I was a lot more interested in him than I might want to admit.

"Who brought you to the party last week?"

I could tell by his expression that this was the last thing he'd expected me to ask. But it had been niggling at me even before I ran into him again. How had he ended up at that party?

"If I tell you, do you promise not to fire them?"

"You think I'd fire them because they brought you to my work function? I don't think *that* badly of you."

"You had me tossed out of your building. Excuse me if I find that difficult to believe."

He had a point. But that would've been a first impulse when I found out I'd been lied to. Now, I was in payback mode.

"I won't fire them. I'm just curious who I have to thank for your presence in my life."

Gabe laughed. "Oh yes, that sounds very convincing."

I liked his laugh. It was joyful, carefree, and rumbled out of him with ease. I also liked the fact that I'd caused that reaction.

"Ryan Carrigan. He works for—"

"Alexander."

Gabe's eyes widened. "You know him?"

"I know all of my employees. Does that surprise you?"

"A little. You don't really strike me as the type who'd know the—" Gabe cut himself off abruptly, but I had a feeling I knew where he was going.

"The type who'd know who?"

He shrugged. "The little fish."

That was an interesting way to put it, and I had a feeling that that was more Ryan talking than Gabe, because the beautiful man sitting beside me had confidence to spare. There was no way he'd ever think of himself as a "little" anything. Hell, he'd come after me with not an ounce of subtlety—and caught me.

"I make sure I know everyone who works at ENN. That's my job. I can't be effective if I'm not aware of what each person brings to the table, and Ryan is a wonderful asset to Alexander."

Gabe grinned. "He'd be shocked to hear you say so."

"Maybe the next time I see him, I'll tell him."

"*No.* Don't do that."

"Why not?"

"Because then he'll know I was talking to you about him. Don't treat him any different to how you always treat him."

"I don't treat him any way at all. I've never spoken to him."

"There." Gabe nodded. "Just keep doing that."

I frowned and gestured to my phone. "Can I have that back now, please?"

Gabe looked to where my cell was peeking out from under his thigh and shook his head. "Nope. We're still talking."

That was what I'd been afraid of. I took a deep breath and tried for patience. "Okay, then talk."

"How long have you been the president of ENN?"

"The last eight years."

"Wow, that's a long time."

"Is it?" It seemed pretty normal for a working professional, and again I wondered exactly how old Gabe was. "You work for Logan, is that right?"

Twin spots of color appeared on his cheeks at the mention of his boss. "Yeah, I just recently started there. Actually, I was hired the day we met."

"Really?"

"Yep. I was out, um, celebrating."

"Well, I hope you a good night."

Gabe grinned. "Oh, I did. Free drinks, good conversation, and it ended it with a bang. What more could I have asked for?"

What more, indeed? Franklin drew the car to a stop outside the ENN building, and I was two seconds away from telling him to drive us around the block when Gabe looked out the window.

"Oh look, we're here. You're finally free of me."

"For now," I said.

"For now."

I released my seatbelt, but before I left, I had one final question for him: "How old are you?"

Gabe reached under his thigh and held out my phone. "Old enough to drink and young enough to get up at four a.m. for the next week to win our little deal—if that's what it takes."

That told me absolutely nothing.

Then he asked, "How old are *you*?"

"Old enough to know trouble when I see it."

"I don't see you looking away…"

Neither did I, and that was when Franklin opened the door.

Gabe chuckled. "Perfect timing, Franklin. You have a wonderful day, Mr. St. James."

I climbed out of the car and took the briefcase Franklin handed me. "If you could please take Mr. Romero wherever he needs to go?"

"Very well, sir."

As Franklin walked off to climb back in the driver's seat, I leaned down and looked inside to Gabe. "Keep your phone on."

He held it up and winked. "I'm available whenever you need me."

The only thing I needed was him naked somewhere, and me inside him. It was as if the more I resisted, the more I wanted him. But it was time to pull back for a moment and regroup. He was getting a little too smug about all of this, and that hadn't been the plan.

I shut the door and walked across the sidewalk to the glass doors of the ENN building, and no one was more shocked than I was to see a smile on the reflection staring back at me.

CHAPTER 16

GABE

"GABE!" LOGAN'S VOICE had me up and out from behind my desk and heading through his office doors as quick as my legs could carry me.

It was closing in on five thirty, and I was currently on my third cup of—what had Marcus called it?—straight black, hard-hitting caffeine. I'd been pretty good up until around two, and then my early-morning call and errand had started to catch up with me.

But I didn't have time to think about how much I'd like to put my head on my desk and close my eyes for five minutes. Logan was getting ready for a big case next week, and he'd been barking orders at me all day. So yeah, it was a great day for me to also be on Marcus's clock.

Speaking of Marcus, I hadn't heard from him since he left me in the back of his SUV earlier this morning. Not that I would've had time to deal with him even if I had. But the fact he hadn't reached out or even sent a text hadn't gone unnoticed. In fact, it had been driving me crazy. Every time I got two seconds to myself, I checked to see if there was anything, and each and every time...nothing.

"Oh good, there you are," Logan said as he looked up from his laptop. "Can you go and get the Markham file off Cole for me? He said he was done with it, and I need to get some information out of it."

"Of course." I went to leave, but Logan spoke up again.

"Also, can you get George Denton's phone number?"

I nodded.

"Oh, and Tate, shit. Hold all of that, would you? I need to call him first. I'm going to be late getting out of here tonight."

Which meant I would be too. Any other day I wouldn't care, because that meant overtime, which meant more money in my empty pockets. Today, however, I barely managed to stifle a yawn.

"You got it," I said as Logan went back to reading whatever was on his screen, and I went back to my desk.

Situated as it was in a section directly outside of Logan's office, I had a clear view of him should he need me, and a view of anyone walking down the hall from the lobby. No one got to him unless it was on my schedule after *he'd* approved it, and I had to wonder what I would've done had someone like myself turned up and tried to get past me the way I had Marcus's PA.

That hadn't been one of my most shining moments, that was for sure. But it'd gotten me what I wanted in the end, sooo I figured it was worth it.

I pulled up George Denton's number and jotted it down, and was about to go and see if Cole was in his office when my cell phone lit up on my desk. As soon as *his* name flashed across the screen, my heart began to thump and I woke up in an instant.

This was crazy. I didn't even really know Marcus other than he was sexy, bossy, and exceedingly self-important. But a single text from him and I lit up like the Fourth of July.

What time are you available for me this evening?

Even though my brain knew he was asking so he could continue with his little payback plan, that was super fucking hot. What time was I *available* for him? I shot back: **Whenever you want me.**

I grinned, wishing I could see the frown that was no doubt marring his brow, as he struggled over the fact that, deep down, he really *did* want me. That was one of the things that turned me on the most about Marcus: his inability to decide whether he wanted to throttle me or fuck me. I knew which option I preferred, but if we had to duke it out first, then I was up for the challenge.

I glanced up to see Logan through the glass walls of his office leaning back in his chair and smiling at the phone. He was clearly on the line with Tate now, and I thought how nice it must be to have a person in your life that could always make you smile.

I was about to go and grab the file off Cole when another message came through that made a shiver of anticipation race up my spine.

What TIME, Gabe?

I gnawed on my lip for a second before I began to write back that I wasn't sure. Then line one on my work phone lit up—Logan. I snatched up the phone and brought it to my ear.

"Change in plans."

I looked through the glass to where he was now on his feet closing his laptop.

"I'm leaving early," he said as he picked up his briefcase and put it on the desk. Then he unfastened it and began placing files inside it.

"So you don't want the Markham file or Denton's number?"

"I already emailed Cole for the file, and I'll grab that number on my way out." He looked up and over at me, and there was a spark in his eyes that only one person could put there—Tate. "It's Friday night, or so I was just reminded. Pack up and go home, Gabe. Do something fun. I plan to."

I wasn't one hundred percent sure, but I was close to positive there was a double meaning in there somewhere. I nodded as Logan shut his briefcase and then hung up the phone.

*Do something fun? Or do some*one...

I picked up my cell, then typed back to Marcus: **I'm at your beck and call, sir. Just tell me what you need.**

Three dots appeared, and I shifted in my seat, my excitement over possibly getting to see him sooner than anticipated making it a little difficult to remain decent.

I'm working late, so I'll need something for dinner. I'll send you over my order. Make sure you're here by six thirty.

Something about that really flicked my switch. **I think you're forgetting something…**

His response was immediate: **And what might that be?**

I'm not allowed in your building anymore. Someone on a power trip recently threw me out.

Lucky for you, someone with the POWER to let you back in is hungry. Be here by six thirty.

This whole *power* conversation had me reaching under the desk and pressing the heel of my hand against my eager dick. There was something to be said for authority and confidence, and Marcus had it in spades.

Logan pulled open his office door and stepped out at that exact moment, and I quickly brought my hand back above the desk.

Yeah, as if *that* didn't look suspicious.

Logan paused in front of me, and I tore the Post-it note free and handed it over.

"Mr. Denton's number."

He took it and folded it before sliding it into the pocket beneath his jacket. Then he gestured to the phone. "Making plans?"

I looked down to see that another message had flashed up on my screen from Marcus, and Logan chuckled.

"The *Almighty?*"

"Uh..." My cheeks heated, then I laughed. "Yeah. It's just a nickname."

"I see." Logan eyed me closely. "Well, I suppose that's convenient for someone whose *own* name slips by him so often."

My mouth fell open. "I thought... You said we were all good about that."

"Oh, we are." Logan gave a crooked smile as he walked backward to the hall. "But you must admit— Oh *God*." He moaned, and my eyes widened as I looked from left to right to see if anyone else was around. "Makes it less embarrassing if you forget his name in the heat of the moment. Have a good weekend, Gabe."

When he winked at me and spun on his Italian leather shoes to walk out into the lobby, I had to pick my jaw up off the floor.

Logan was always so professional around me, and we were still trying to find our footing with each other. But that was the first time he'd ever said anything *that* personal, and holy shit, the man was hot when he moaned like he was— Well, he was just hot. I sometimes forgot that, since I'd been careful to shove him in the boss box.

When my phone flashed again with a notification, however, I allowed the delicious feel of anticipation and exhilaration to wash over me, because there was a man I didn't have to hold back around.

CHAPTER 17

MARCUS

THE KNOCKING ON my office door went hand in hand with the headache forming behind my eyes. I looked at the clock sitting on my desk. Six twenty-five—he was right on time. Or should I say that Carmen, trying to decide whether I'd lost my mind or not, was on time. I called out for her to enter.

She gingerly pushed open the door and stepped inside. "Sorry to interrupt you, sir, but I just received a call from downstairs that the man from yesterday who was removed from your office is back."

"Yes, I'm aware. I invited him."

"You invited him?"

"Yes. He's bringing me dinner."

"The man you...threw out yesterday?"

"That's correct."

"Uh..."

This was the first time I'd ever seen Carmen falter with

me. She'd survived so long as my PA because of her intellect and superior work ethic. Right now, she looked completely dumbfounded, and I couldn't blame her. Not one little bit.

"It's okay, Carmen. His name is Gabe, and we worked out our misunderstanding. You can let him up."

She still looked as though she thought I was mad, and maybe I was, but I couldn't seem to find it in me to care. I knew the smart thing to do was to call this all off, to tell Gabe that everything was forgiven and nip this in the bud. But the idea of not seeing him again or hearing his smart mouth talk back to me didn't sit well with me.

Around five minutes later, a second—much louder—knock came. As the door pushed open, I found myself holding my breath waiting for Gabe to enter. When he did, I was reminded of the exact reason I couldn't end this. It was that draw, that magnetic pull whenever he was near—it struck like lightning as his gaze found mine from across the wide expanse of the office. Then he held up two plastic bags and inclined his head like some sort of manservant.

"Your dinner, Mr. St. James."

As he closed the door behind him, I reached for my phone and hit Carmen's line. "Carmen?"

"Yes, sir?"

With my eyes still locked with Gabe's, I said into the phone, "You can go home for the night."

He smirked, and my dick stiffened at the arrogant expression, as he strolled into my office as though he hadn't been tossed out of it the day before.

"Are you sure?" Carmen asked. "I can wait until—"

"I'm sure," I said, my attention never straying from Gabe. "I don't know how much longer I'll be, and I'm sure you have other plans. Have a good night."

I effectively ended the call for her, and as I did, I sat back in my seat and let my eyes rove over Gabe.

"You're on time."

"I can follow an order." The wicked glint in his eyes made it clear he was not talking about schedules. Before this got out of control, I gestured to the bags.

"Did you find the place okay?"

"I did. They have this wonderful thing called the internet. I'm not sure if you've heard of it, since you probably just have other people look things up for you."

There was that smart mouth. Maybe that was it, the reason I was so drawn to him. Gabe had absolutely no issues talking back to me. He didn't walk around on eggshells either, and that was...exciting.

"Where would you like me?" he said, and my cock had several suggestions about that. Then he jiggled the bags and added, "To put *this*?"

I dragged my eyes away from his and gestured to the coffee table in front of the couch. "Over there will be fine."

All day I'd thought about this moment, when he would be back within touching distance, back within view, and it had taken everything I had not to call him over here at lunch. As he placed the bags down and shrugged out of his jacket, I sat forward in my chair to get a better look at him. He unbuttoned his shirt sleeves and rolled them up his thick, tanned forearms. When that silver bracelet came into view, I was on my feet and around the desk before I knew what I was doing.

When he sensed my approach, he turned and sucked in a swift breath.

Gabe craned his head back to look me in the eye, and it took everything I had not to reach out and sweep the longer strands of his hair back from his gorgeous face.

He bit down into his lip and raised the container between the two of us. "Hungry?"

"Starving."

He swallowed and gestured to the food. "Then you should eat."

I couldn't have agreed more. But suddenly the food in the boxes was the last thing I wanted in my mouth.

Gabe picked up a paper plate and a set of utensils, then held them out to me. I took them from him and ordered myself to step away, then I pointed to the food. "Do you like soul food?"

Gabe looked at the vast array of containers he'd set out, and then back to me. "I've never had it."

"Never?"

He shook his head, and I gestured to the other empty plates on the table. "That changes tonight. Get yourself a plate."

"That's fine. I—"

"Have you eaten?" I figured the answer to that was a no, since I'd had him go directly from work to Solé to pick up my meal, which was why I'd ordered enough for two.

"No, but—"

"Then get yourself a plate."

Gabe looked as though he wanted to argue some more, but caved. Good. I wouldn't have him go hungry.

"This here," I said, pointing to the large serving of shrimp, "is their New Orleans-style barbecue shrimp. It's buttery and spicy, and—"

"I'm allergic to shellfish."

I stopped in my tracks, that thought never having occurred to me. I glanced over to see Gabe's lips twitch with undisguised mirth. That little shit—he was trying to throw me off my game.

"In that case, eat ten of them."

He burst out laughing. "Ouch, that's harsh. Even from you."

I shook my head and moved down the table. "If you manage to survive the *shrimp*, this is their blackened catfish. It's served with dirty rice and is flavored to perfection."

"High praise."

"It's well deserved." I plated some shrimp and then the fish and rice, before taking a seat on the couch.

When Gabe did the same but remained standing, I looked to the spot beside me. "I don't bite."

He pursed his lips for a moment and then moved to take the seat. "I wasn't worried about you."

A smirk pulled at my lips, and Gabe grinned.

"Ah ha! Finally," he said.

"What?"

"You smiled."

"That wasn't a smile."

"Well"—he pointed at my mouth—"your lips did something other than grimace, so I'm going to take the victory whether you want to give it to me or not."

"Fair enough. But it wasn't a smile."

Gabe shrugged and settled into the couch. "Okay, Mr. Serious. Here's a question for you. Do you always eat dinner in your office on a Friday night?"

I took a bite of the shrimp and enjoyed the spicy flavors. "No, last Friday I had scorching-hot sex in the studio downstairs."

Gabe's eyes darkened and he shifted in his seat, then he turned away from me, seeming to need a second to gather himself. When he caught the view of the lake in front of him, the sheer beauty of it seemed to push all other thoughts aside. His mouth fell open and he looked out to the lake below. "Jesus, how do you get anything done when you sit and stare at that all day?"

I speared another shrimp with my fork and looked over at the windows. "At first it was difficult, but now—"

"You're too busy to notice?"

The glib comment wasn't a shock; most people assumed I took for granted the luxuries I was afforded—the house, the car, the fancy office—but I never did. It had taken too much hard work and too many years of being committed to my job to get where I was.

But I wasn't stupid, I knew it could all be gone tomorrow. Success was hard to get, but it was even harder to keep.

"No. *Now*, instead of awe, I find comfort in it." I could feel Gabe's eyes on me, but didn't look away from the view.

"When everything is going crazy up here, and the world seems to be falling apart, I look out there and gain a sense of peace. I'm reminded that there is beauty in the world, even on the darkest days. And trust me, in this job, there are some very dark days."

The room fell silent, and I turned to look at my dinner companion.

"Wow," he said.

"This job isn't an easy one, and it demands a *lot* of my time. But despite what you think or have been told, I do find pleasure in things beyond it."

Gabe shifted on the couch until he was facing me. "Like what? What do you like to do for fun?"

The question was so normal, so common between two people getting to know one another. But it had been so long since I'd actually taken the time and effort to do so that the words felt extremely personal.

Gabe took a bite of his shrimp as he waited, and as the rich flavors burst inside his mouth, he groaned.

"Oh my God, you were right," he said around a mouthful. "This is delicious."

And so was he. Everything about him. His smile, his laugh, those tempting, full lips of his. Gabriel Romero made me hungry for things I'd never wanted, and starved of the things I didn't think I would ever need.

"Sorry," he said, wiping at his lips. "You were saying?"

He picked up a second piece of shrimp, and before I knew it, the words "Come and stay with me this weekend" tumbled out of my mouth.

CHAPTER 18
GABE

I COULDN'T BE sure, but I was almost positive that Marcus had just asked me to stay with him this weekend—at his *house*. But as I sat beside him with a piece of shrimp between my fingers, he remained silent.

There was no follow-up, no explanation, just silence, and before I answered, I wanted to make sure I hadn't misheard him.

"You want me to—"

"Come and stay with me? Yes."

He was so matter-of-fact about it that for a second I just sat there, my brain trying to comprehend how the sexiest man I'd ever met had just asked me to come and play house with him.

He added, "It makes the most sense. I don't know what I'll need, you still have a deal to fulfill, and my house has more than enough bedrooms and bathrooms that you'll find yourself comfortable, I'm sure."

Oh, okay. That made more sense. He wanted me close so I could tend to his every whim. I should've known better. But that might also work in my favor. It would be so much easier to torture and tempt him if I was close by. It was clear the desire was still there. I'd seen the way he'd been watching me tonight. I'd also noticed him loosening up a little—if you could call it that. He was letting me in a little more every time I was around, and I couldn't pass up the offer to learn even more.

I popped the scrumptious piece of shrimp in my mouth, swallowed it, then nodded. "Okay. I'll come." One of Marcus's brows winged up, and I chuckled. I knew exactly where his mind had just gone. He wasn't fooling anyone, certainly not me, and I wouldn't let him think he was.

I knew when someone was interested, and despite his cool exterior, Marcus was hot for me. "I have one condition, though," I said.

"And that is?"

"I want you to show me something you do for fun."

His eyes narrowed as I picked up another piece of shrimp. Damn, this stuff was good. "Can't I just tell you?"

I shook my head. "Nope. I want to see what *the* Marcus St. James considers fun."

"And if I don't agree?"

"Then I won't come this weekend."

Marcus eyed me for several pulse-pounding seconds then said, "We both know that's not true."

I slicked my tongue over my lower lip. "Okay. I won't come...with you."

"I thought that offer was off the table?"

"There is such a thing as renegotiation, isn't there?"

The flames flickering in his eyes made the temperature in the room rise several scorching degrees.

"Fine. You have a deal." Marcus slid his plate onto the coffee table and turned to look at me. "You stay the weekend, and I'll show you something I like to do for fun."

Feeling victorious, I grinned and pointed at him. "See, what was so hard about that?"

Quick as whip, Marcus's hand shot out, and he grabbed my wrist, tugging me forward. "Currently—me. But that was your plan since the second you saw me, wasn't it?"

I refocused my attention on his lap, and true to his words, Marcus was hard as a rock inside his pants. The sexual tension vibrated between us as we sat there, inches from each other. My breathing was ragged, my pulse was racing, and *my* cock was now pounding as hard as my heart.

"Say you agree, Gabe. Say that you'll come and stay."

As if I was going to say anything else. "I agree."

"Good," he said, then he slowly brought my hand up and flicked his tongue over one of my fingertips.

Oh shit. Shiiit. It was a simple gesture, but an overtly sexual one. He sucked the buttery tip between his lips and swirled his tongue around it. When he finally raised his head, he released my wrist before picking his plate back up.

"I'm glad we got that sorted out."

"Me too," I managed to say, knowing that if I hoped to wield any kind of power in this dynamic, I had to keep my wits about me. "So...um, will Franklin be stopping by my house so I can pick up some clothes? Or am I just expected to parade around naked all weekend?"

Marcus finished his mouthful of fish. "I'm sure he'll be happy to make the stop."

I settled back into the couch, thinking it was probably a smart idea to move away. Then I started in on the rest of my meal. The food really was fantastic—I could see why Marcus was a fan—and we each ate the rest of our dinner in a comfortable but tense silence.

Once we were done, Marcus reached for my plate. "Here, let me take that for you."

"Uh ah." I sprang to my feet. "I am here to do things for *you*, remember? I can't find myself in more debt once this is done."

Marcus frowned. "This doesn't count."

"Yes it does." As I began to clean up the plates, Marcus put his hand over the now-empty serving dish and shook his head.

"*I'll* clean up."

"Really, it's okay. I'm sure you have work to do."

"It can wait." His tone was not to be argued with. "I don't want you cleaning up after me, Gabe. That wasn't part of our deal."

I froze, about to tell him I was cleaning up after myself, but he slowly got to his feet. He took the plates out of my hand and began to clear the table, and I let him do what he wanted.

Marcus was an interesting one, that was for sure. He had a person for practically everything, and yet he balked at the idea of me picking up a bit of trash? Oh well, at least this gave me the opportunity to look around a little.

I made my way over to the windows and looked down at the pretty city lights and boats dotting the lake. It really was a spectacular view, and I knew it must've taken years to achieve the kind of prestige and recognition Marcus had to be given a space like this to work in.

I turned to watch him and felt a rush I knowing that he was taking time out of what had to be an insane schedule to talk to me, to...*be* with me.

I mean, yeah, he would've had to eat whether I was here or not. But he could've just had me drop it off. He didn't have to invite me to stay.

Marcus walked over to the trash can by the door and put the tied bags inside, then he made his way back across the office, and I took a moment to enjoy *this* view. His tailored pants made his legs look longer than they already were, and with his jacket open, I could see the fit, trim body that his crisp shirt outlined underneath.

Damn. I'd felt that body along the front and back of mine, and I had every intention of feeling it there again.

Marcus rounded his desk and pressed a few buttons on his computer, then he glanced at me.

"I'm going to shut down here for the night so we can head by your place and collect your things."

"I don't have that many."

He shut his computer and reached for his briefcase. "Bring as little or as much as you like. There's plenty of room."

I didn't doubt it. His place was huge. I just didn't want to take up his time. I knew how busy he was.

"Also"—he paused as he came to a stop by me—"I don't want you to think that by you staying with me that I expect—"

"Sex?" Marcus's jaw ticked, and I took a step toward him, bold as ever, just like the night we met. "What if I do?"

His eyes roved over my face, and I angled my chin up to give him a better look. From the very beginning I'd been nothing but shameless in my pursuit of him, and I wouldn't hold back now.

"Gabe."

Oh, hell yes. I *loved* the way he said my name like that. All growly.

"We should go." Marcus stepped aside and gestured for the door. "I believe you know the way to the elevators."

I sure did, and my ass moved quicker than you could blink in the direction of the door.

CHAPTER 19

MARCUS

THE TRIP TO Gabe's wasn't a long one. Franklin had us across town and at the entrance of the apartment building in under ten minutes. But with the tension simmering between us, those ten minutes had felt like ten hours.

I couldn't remember the last time I'd had to physically restrain myself from reaching out and touching someone. But I almost had to sit on my hands. Gabe was testing every ounce of control I had, and he knew it.

"This is me," he said as Franklin drew to a stop, then Gabe reached for the door and pushed it open. When I did the same thing, he froze. "What are you doing?"

"Coming with you."

"Oh, well, I'm not going to take long."

"That's okay. I don't mind walking you up."

"Uh, you don't have—"

"Is there a reason you don't want me to come with you?"

He'd told me he was single the night of the party. I hoped at least that part was true.

Gabe's brow furrowed and he opened his mouth then shook his head. "No, you should come up. As long as Franklin won't get lonely."

I caught Franklin's eyes in the mirror, and he raised a brow. "Franklin's just fine. Now, let's go."

We headed inside a small but nice lobby and made our way to the elevators. When we hit the tenth floor and stepped out, Gabe made a left and started down the hall. When we were about halfway there, he stopped and put a hand on my arm.

"I have to tell you something before we get to my place."

So I hadn't been wrong—something was definitely bothering him about me coming up here with him. "Okay, so tell me."

"I have a roommate, and he may or may not be home."

I didn't see an issue with that, unless... "Is he *just* a roommate?"

"Oh, definitely. But...you know him."

"Mr. Carrigan."

"Right."

I could see how that might be a problem. "Would you like me to wait out here?"

"No." Gabe shook his head. "I just wanted to let you know in case he's home and he acts a little...weird."

"A little weird?"

"Well, yeah. It's not every day your boss's boss comes to your house, and you're kind of the biggest boss around."

"The *biggest* boss?"

"You know what I mean."

"Yes, I just liked hearing you say it."

Gabe rolled his eyes and walked off ahead of me, and something about that indifference to who I was and what I did in this town was supremely attractive. I followed behind, not upset in the slightest, since he hadn't bothered replacing his jacket, and the fitted shirt and pants did phenomenal things to his tight, compact body.

What I wouldn't give to see him stretched out naked in my bed.

"This is it," he said, glancing over his shoulder, and his smirk told me I'd just been caught looking.

Not bothered in the least, I slipped my hands in my pockets and waited for him to unlock the door.

"Hey, you. I wasn't sure if you'd be home tonight or out doing some kind of menial task for the Almi—"

"Ry! *Heeey*," Gabe said, cutting Ryan off before he could finish his sentence. "Marcus gave me a lift home so I could collect some clothes for the weekend."

"*Marcus?*" Ryan said as though he'd never spoken my name out loud before.

"Yeah." Gabe stepped aside, and I walked through the door. "He's right here, *with* me."

Ryan sprang to his feet like his ass had caught on fire. "M...Marcus," he said, and had he not looked so uncomfortable, I might've laughed, but I feared that would only confuse him more.

"Mr. Carrigan. I apologize for the intrusion."

Ryan shook his head. "No intrusion, Mr. St. James. You don't have to apologize. You're the boss."

That made my lips twitch. "Not here, I'm not."

"Oh." Still wide-eyed and no doubt trying to work out why I was standing in his living room, Ryan turned to Gabe. "Can I, um, see you for a minute?"

One glance at Gabe and his cheeky dimples told me he was enjoying this moment. "Sure. Did you want to go to the kitchen, or—"

Ryan shoved Gabe toward a door just off the front of the room. "Your bedroom will work fine."

The word *bedroom* in correlation to Gabe did things to my body that were out of my hands, and I was glad the two men were leaving so I could try to get it under some kind of control.

As they disappeared behind a door, I took a second to look around. Their place was nice, quiet, minimalistic, which I appreciated. It was neat as a pin, too. But then, Ryan was always very well put together whenever I saw him, so that wasn't all that shocking. The space wasn't big, but it was comfortable enough for two. It reminded me of the first apartment I lived in when I moved out of home, and didn't that bring to light the difference between Gabe and myself?

From our age to our occupations and everything in between, nothing about Gabe should feel right. Yet he was the first person in years that I'd bothered to stop and look at outside of work—and I *was* looking.

I was looking so hard that I'd invited him to stay at my

house. Yes, I'd done it under false pretenses, but I'd invited him just the same. Because the moment he reappeared in my life after that first night, I'd seen an opportunity to keep him near and snatched it up with two greedy hands.

I stared at the door and wondered what exactly was being said behind it. No doubt something along the lines of *Are you insane?* And I couldn't blame Ryan. None of this made any sense, and yet I wasn't going to stop it.

Gabe was an adult; it was his decision what he did or didn't want to do, and he'd made it loud and clear back in my office that he was comfortable with this new facet of our deal.

Just as that thought entered my mind, the door reopened and Ryan walked out. He looked at me and offered up a polite—if strained—smile.

"Gabe's just finishing packing a bag. Would you like something to drink?"

I could tell Ryan was rattled by my presence, unsure how he should act around his boss outside of the workplace. So I nodded, to give him something to do.

"A water would be great, thank you."

He nodded and hurried off toward the kitchen, and I followed him across the room, stopping on the opposite side of a small island. Like the rest of the apartment, the space wasn't large, but it was big enough to be comfortable. It was all white tile and stainless steel. Ryan slid a glass of iced water my way, and I smiled and thanked him.

"Um, you're welcome," he said before moving back a

step and standing still as a statue, as though he were under observation.

"You can relax." I took a sip and looked at him over the rim of the glass.

"No offense, but that's kind of impossible. You're standing in my kitchen."

"Exactly. We aren't at work, so there's no need to feel—"

"Awkward as hell?"

I chuckled and took another sip. "Right."

"Sorry to break it to you, but whether we're at work or you're standing in my kitchen drinking a glass of water, you're still Alexander's boss, who is my boss. Therefore, I'm on my best behavior."

I nodded. "Fair enough. But let me ask you this: if I wasn't Alexander's boss, what would you be saying right now instead?"

Ryan eyed me, and I could tell he had plenty to say about me showing up here. I wondered if he'd be brave enough to actually say it.

"I'd ask what the hell you're doing with my best friend."

That answered that. I lowered my glass to the counter and eyed him closely. His back was ramrod straight, belying the relaxed fit of the shorts and shirt he'd swapped his suit for when he arrived home.

"Right now? Giving him a lift home so he can pack a bag."

Ryan narrowed his eyes and took a step toward the island. "That's not what I mean, and you know it."

I did, and while I knew he was looking out for his friend,

what I planned to do with Gabe was none of Ryan's business.

"We're all adults, the three of us, are we not?"

"We are."

"Then I think you understand exactly what I'm doing with Gabe."

Ryan scoffed, and just like that, the polite work version of him flew out the window. "Don't try that bullshit with me. Gabe told me all about your deal and how you're making him 'pay off' his little lie."

"Little?" I shook my head. "He told me he was someone else. Someone I later had a very important work meeting with. That's hardly little. But yes, I felt this was the least he could do to *pay off* his transgressions."

Ryan crossed his arms, adopting a defensive posture. "And let me guess, his final order will be to get in your bed?"

"If it is and he does, that would be his choice, wouldn't it?"

"Oh, don't even try with that. Do you really think for one second that someone like you couldn't seduce him?"

It was all I could do not to laugh. "Have you met your friend? Have you *seen* him? I'm not sure what Gabe told you about the night we met and what happened, but I wasn't the one doing the seducing."

Ryan rolled his eyes, but I could tell by his expression that he knew I was telling the truth. Gabe was a heartbreaker and Ryan knew it. From his confidence to his smile, those dimples and his sexy smirk, if he turned that charm on you, there wasn't a person alive who wouldn't cave—including, apparently, me.

Ryan tried a different tactic: "Don't you think he's a little bit young for you?"

It should've worked, too. I'd been telling myself the same thing, but for some reason, I was undeterred. I'd never set out to find myself a boy toy. That wasn't for me. But I'd be damned if something about Gabe's youth and vitality didn't make me remember how to…let go a little.

"Now you're grasping. But since you went down that path, I have no idea. He hasn't told me how old he is. All he said was that he was legal. So unless that's a lie—"

"It's not."

"Then everything *after* that is just a number." Or so I kept telling myself. "What's the real problem here, Ryan?"

Ryan ground his teeth together. "I don't want you to hurt him. To…*use* him."

There was that word again.

"Gabe's a good guy, and he only lied because he wanted to talk to you, and I said—" Ryan stopped abruptly, and his eyes shifted over my shoulder.

"Should I even *ask* what you two are talking about?" Gabe said.

My body went on high alert. My blood started pumping a little harder and my pulse began to race, and I didn't care what anybody had to say about what we were doing. I was taking Gabe home this weekend, and whatever happened happened.

I turned, ready to get going, but when I saw him

standing in the center of the room in a pair of worn jeans and a loose black linen shirt that he'd left half unbuttoned, I came to a dead stop. He'd done something to his hair so it was styled just like *that* night. As he hiked his overnight bag up his shoulder, the lights caught on the silver necklace around his neck.

He looked sexy and relaxed, and I couldn't tear my eyes away from him. He knew it, too, judging by the half-smile on his lips. He came to a stop just inches from me, then looked to Ryan and waved.

"See you Sunday night."

"Monday," I corrected him. "You'll see him Monday night. Sunday is part of the weekend, and that's mine."

He licked along his bottom lip, and I wanted to grab him and bite it.

"Monday night, then. See you, Ry."

If Ryan said anything in return, I didn't hear him. I was too busy trying to keep my hands to myself as Gabe walked ahead of me toward the door. I'd almost convinced myself we'd make it to the elevator and down to the car when the door shut behind us and I lost the battle.

CHAPTER 20

GABE

THE SECOND THE door to my apartment shut, Marcus grabbed the strap of my bag and tugged me around on the spot.

Before I could begin to process what Marcus was about, he had my back up against the wall and him against my front, and the thick, hard press of his erection against mine made me groan with desire.

When I'd stepped into the living room and seen him and Ryan in the kitchen, I worried that my roommate had been trying to talk Marcus out of this deal we'd entered into. I knew he was convinced I was going to get hurt, and was extra freaked out now that I was going to stay with Marcus for the weekend. But nothing other than a natural disaster was going to keep me from leaving with Marcus.

I dropped my bag to the floor and reached for Marcus's hips. He angled my face up toward his, and my fingers dug into his ass.

"What the hell are you doing to me?" he whispered over the top of my lips.

"Pretty sure you grabbed me, buuut..." I flexed my fingers, and Marcus's grip tightened.

"I need to know: are you sure you want to come with me this weekend?"

"Is that a trick question?"

"I'm being serious, Gabe."

I could see that. Damn Ryan—despite what I could feel happening below Marcus's waist, my do-gooder friend had definitely gotten in his head. Well, time to change that.

I pulled Marcus in and ground my hips against his. "I wouldn't be here if I didn't want to come." Marcus's eyes flared, and lust swirled there. "And I'd much rather do that with you than alone, *thinking* about you."

"That isn't the deal we made."

"No, but I told you, I'm open to renegotiation. You are too."

"Jesus." Marcus took my lips in a savage kiss full of need and frustration. I groaned and opened up to him, and he took my face with both hands and dove in for a deeper taste. Our tongues tangled, and when he wedged a foot between mine and pressed his thigh up between my legs, my hips began to move as though I was naked and he was inside me.

I was burning up, right there in the hall. When Marcus kissed his way up to my ear, my hips began to move even faster.

"You look and smell like a fucking fantasy—like *my* fantasy."

My head fell back against the wall, my breathing coming hard now. I needed more friction. I needed to be naked. But just as that thought entered my mind, Marcus let out a sigh and slowly stepped away.

God, he was sexy. His lips were swollen, his eyes were as dark as I'd ever seen them, and as I greedily took in his tall, powerful frame, I reached down and massaged myself. "Why'd you stop?"

Marcus lowered his eyes to my hand. "Because the next time I'm inside you, it's not going to be against a wall."

Well, that sounded promising. "So there'll definitely *be* a next time."

"If you keep getting yourself off in front of me like you are, there'll be a right now time—on the floor."

I looked to the carpet and then back to him, but Marcus shook his head.

"No."

"But—"

"No."

Before I could say another word, he started off toward the elevator, and I couldn't help but laugh. Okay, he hadn't said that there wouldn't be a next time, so I guessed I'd behave for now.

But later tonight, I would be coming for that man…in *all* the ways.

. . .

BY THE TIME we climbed back into the Escalade, my body was under some kind of control and Marcus was back to work. He had his phone out and was emailing, calling, and texting God knew who, and it gave me the perfect opportunity to study him in his element.

With his lips pulled into a stern, serious line, his eyes narrowed on what he was reading, the slight tic in his jaw made me think he was either concentrating or annoyed.

It was easy to see how a person could be intimidated by him when he was in work mode. But all I saw was a man who was dedicated to his career and worked hard every minute of the day.

I could appreciate that even with such differences between us, because I knew that to get to where I eventually wanted to be, I was going to have to work even harder than I'd first anticipated. But I didn't want to think about that tonight. I wanted to think about the fact that I was about to spend the next two days and three nights in this man's company.

"You're unusually quiet over there," Marcus said as he slipped his phone inside his pocket and Franklin pulled onto his street.

"You needed to work, and I didn't want to disturb you."

"That's thoughtful of you."

"You sound surprised."

"I am. I don't think you've been silent in my presence since the moment I met you."

"Is that a complaint?"

"No. Just an observation. You're very...energetic."

That made me laugh. "Is that a subtle way of saying *young*?"

"No, it's my way of saying you're energetic. But to that point, you *are* young."

"I never hid that."

"No, you didn't. But you definitely portrayed yourself as older when we first met. Didn't you?"

"Maybe a little, but I didn't think you'd look twice at me if you knew I was twenty-two."

"Twenty-two." Marcus's voice was eerily calm as his eyes narrowed, and I wasn't surprised. That was the reaction I figured I'd get when he heard the actual number.

He said nothing more as the SUV came to a stop, then he shoved open the passenger door and climbed out, heading for his home.

I quickly followed suit and watched as he marched up the short path and stairs to the front door. Once we were both inside, he whirled around and said, "Twenty fucking *two?* Are you out of your mind?"

I opened my mouth to respond, but before I could get a word out, Marcus was off again. He stormed across the marble floor of his foyer and down the hall directly ahead of him.

There was no chance to take in my surroundings as we entered what had to be his office. Then he tossed his briefcase on the floor and turned to see me standing just inside the door.

He looked fuming mad. His jaw was clenched, his hands were on his hips, and the fulminating expression on his face should've had me running. But instead, I slowly closed the door.

"You knew I was younger than you."

"I didn't know you were twenty *years* younger than me. I'm forty-two, did you know that?"

"Yes."

"And that doesn't bother you?"

"No, it doesn't."

"Well, it should."

I walked across the room, and Marcus tracked me like a caged animal. One that knew it shouldn't pounce but was dying to anyway.

"The fact that you're older than me is one of the reasons I wanted you in the first place." His jaw ticked beneath his short beard as I stopped opposite him. "Don't act like a number changes the way you feel about me. I can see it in your eyes. You want me just as much now as you did back at my apartment when you had no clue."

"Which is a mistake."

I looked down to his tie and reached out to stroke my thumb over the silky end. "If it is, then it'll be one damn good mistake."

Marcus took hold of my hand and yanked me in until the tips of our shoes met. The irritation and arousal swirling in his eyes made adrenaline rush through my veins, and I braced myself for whatever was about to happen next.

"You should've told me."

The delicious scent of his cologne swirled around me as I stared into his eyes. Marcus was such an attractive man that even pissed off, he was hot.

"I didn't *not* tell you," I said.

"You said you were a lawyer."

"And you found out yesterday that that wasn't true. So who are you really angry at? Me or you?"

Marcus's fingers tightened around my wrist. "You are a beautiful, troublemaking liar."

"I only lied that night," I said, and flicked my tongue over his lips. "And I'd do it all again if it got me back here."

Marcus yanked me forward and took my mouth in a fierce kiss. It was angry and rough, and I loved every damn second of it. He bit and sucked at my lips before thrusting his tongue inside. I groaned and braced myself against his muscled chest, and the sexy sound that rumbled out of him was filled with pent up need.

He released my arm and took my face between his hands. As he angled his head and continued to devour me, he shifted us and began to walk me back into his desk.

I tore my lips free and looked behind me, and when I saw the surface was clear, I moved up onto it. When I was in place, I looked at him from beneath my lashes, and his tense expression made my cock throb.

"We made a deal," he said, as I parted my legs and placed my hands on the desk behind me.

"So you're going to stop? Really?"

Marcus stepped between my thighs and leaned down until his hands were on the flat surface beside mine.

"Yes. *I'm* going to stop. But you…" He let his sizzling-hot gaze rove down to my hard-on. "You're going to keep going. You're going to use *me*."

CHAPTER 21

MARCUS

I WAS OUT of my mind—that much was clear as I stared down into heated amber eyes and popped open the button of Gabe's jeans.

Perched on my desk with his legs spread wide, he was an invitation I could no longer refuse, no matter how many years separated us. I slowly dragged his zipper down, and when Gabe's hips arched up toward me, I slipped my hand inside the denim. His moan made my cock jerk, and I curled my fingers around him and gave a firm pull.

"I'm going to go and take a seat over there, and you should...make yourself comfortable."

Gabe's grin was downright wicked as I removed my hand and watched him get to his feet. Then I took a seat in my leather desk chair and adjusted myself so my dick didn't feel as though it were about to be strangled.

Gabe groaned, but then hooked his thumbs in his jeans and quickly shoved them and his briefs to mid-thigh. That night in the studio there hadn't been time to really look at him, to really *enjoy* him. But he stood before me now, his thick erection free, and I'd be damned if I wasn't going to see *all* of him.

"Unbutton your shirt."

Gabe reached for the bottom button and did as he was told. As his shirt parted to reveal smooth, bronzed skin, I ground my molars together and prayed for patience. But then he shrugged out of it completely, dropped it to the ground, and blew that prayer straight to hell.

He was fucking gorgeous standing there in my office, naked save for the jeans barely clinging to his strong thighs. He had toned arms and rippling abs, and a tattoo across his right ribcage, some sort of musical composition. My hands itched with the need to trace it.

I wanted to kiss, touch, and suck every single part of him, and suddenly the last thing on my mind was his age.

"Lose the jeans."

Gabe swallowed but showed zero hesitancy as he kicked out of his shoes and shoved the rest of his clothing down his legs. Once he was free and standing tall, I heard myself say, "Come here."

A triumphant smile stretched his full lips as he walked over. I spread my legs, and he stepped in between them. I reached out and traced a fingertip down his muscled thigh.

"I wanted to see you like this the night of the party." Gabe trembled as my finger followed the same path back up. "Naked, hard, greedy..."

My fingers flirted with the dark crop of curls around the root of his dick, and his hips lurched forward.

"Know what else I wanted?" I wrapped my hand around him and moved to my feet. Gabe took in a seriously shaky breath. "I wanted to watch your face when you came."

"Fuck." Gabe placed a hand on my arm to steady himself as I slowly started to stroke him. He began to roll his hips, sliding his cock in and out of my fist, and I growled.

"Mmm, that's it." I angled his chin up so his eyes were on mine. "Use me."

Gabe's fingers dug into my forearm as he rocked his hips a little faster, and I squeezed and stroked him in time to his thrusts. There was a sexy flush staining his cheeks, and he was biting into his lower lip as he fucked my fist with greedy desperation.

I reached for the back of his neck and pulled him in to take his mouth with mine. He wound one of his legs around my thigh, and I sucked his lower lip in between mine as he pumped his hips back and forth, rubbing himself all over me.

He was making a hell of a mess of my pants, but in that moment, I didn't fucking care. I wanted him to come all over them, and I wanted to watch him while he did it.

"Marcus," he said as he tore his lips free. I lowered my mouth to the strong column of his throat and licked his Adam's apple as I swiped my thumb over the sticky head of his dick. Gabe's fingers dug into the sleeve of my jacket, and I wouldn't have been surprised if he'd left holes in it.

He was close—I could feel his body vibrating—and

when I kissed my way up under his ear and sucked, he shoved his hips forward and tensed in my arms.

"Do it," I said by his ear. "Come for me, Gabe, right here in my office. You know you're dying to."

His eyes flew open and blazed to life. Then, with one final punch of his hips, his lips parted and he shouted my name. The next thing I knew he was coming all over my hand in a hot rush of pleasure, and it was the sexiest thing I'd ever seen in my life.

He was the sexiest thing I'd ever seen in my life.

"Wow." He licked his swollen lips as he shivered in my arms. "That was—"

"The hottest fucking thing I've seen in a very long time."

Uncaring of his nudity—and why wouldn't he be?—Gabe wound his arms around my neck, plastering his body up against mine. "Yeah?"

I grabbed his ass and thrust my erection up against his softening one. "What do you think?"

"I think that for the next part of your house tour, you should show me where you sleep."

His audacity, considering he was completely naked, was, as always, one of Gabe's most attractive features.

"I don't think so."

He grinned and rocked against me a little harder. "Are you really not going to let me take care of this for you?"

Against all common sense, I said, "I'm really not. Not while we have this agreement between us."

"Then why don't we cancel it?"

I laughed and shook my head. "No. You owe me a week. I'm not done collecting."

"Not done torturing me, is more like it."

"I hardly think you stripping naked and coming all over me is torture. Torture would've been for me to walk away right *before* you came."

Gabe let me go and picked up his jeans. "Could you have done that?"

"No, which is exactly why you came." I scooped his shirt up and held it out to him, and as he shrugged back into it, I almost wished I'd held on to it. It was such a shame to cover him up.

I picked up a tissue and wiped off my hand. He was finally looking around the room he'd commanded since the second he set foot in it. Like the rest of the house, my office had been lovingly restored to its original state. There were beautiful built-in bookcases, a fireplace at one end with a seat resting in front of it, and a large window that overlooked one of the small courtyards outside. My desk sat at the opposite end of the room, overlooking it all.

It was peaceful in here. I got a lot of work done. But I had a feeling the next time I was in this room, I was going to be one hundred percent distracted.

"I like this space," Gabe said. "It's cozy."

"Uh huh."

He glanced over his shoulder at me. "What? You don't think it is?"

"I do, but right now, 'cozy' is the last word I'd use." I walked past him, careful not to touch him now that my body was back under control, and headed to the door. "Come on, I'll show you where you're going to sleep."

Gabe let out a sigh. "I assume it's a different place to where *you're* going to sleep? Oh well, as long as it has a shower, I guess that's one thing it'll have going for it."

"It does have a shower."

"Want to join me in it?"

More than I wanted my next breath. "Go and get your bag, Gabe, and meet me at the stairs."

The sound of his laughter was all I heard as he walked up the hall, and I couldn't help but wonder what the hell I thought I was doing. One thing was for sure—keeping my distance wasn't it.

CHAPTER 22

GABE

LAST NIGHT HAD been one of the best night's sleep I'd ever had, and I chalked that up to two things. First, the guest room Marcus had put me in had a bed the size of a basketball court. Not to mention a mattress and sheets that were as soft as the clouds in the sky. And two, I'd been coming down from one of the best orgasms of my life.

Just thinking about it now, as I stretched my naked body beneath the sheets, made every single nerve ending come alive and greet the morning. There was a familiar ache between my legs where my erection throbbed, and I couldn't keep my hands off it as I thought about the way Marcus had kissed me goodnight and then ordered me to bed.

He'd told me his room was three doors down if I should need him, and while my body definitely had, I'd given him a reprieve for the night, deciding that I could work on him again this morning.

Not wanting to wait any longer, I threw the covers back,

choosing to go and find him, as opposed to just lying here on my own thinking about him.

I grabbed the plush robe I'd found last night and made my way to the opulent bathroom that accompanied this suite. Marcus had told me that anything I might need should be in the cupboards under the sink. But the first thing I packed last night had been all the necessary items I needed to make sure I didn't look a hot mess.

I mean, a weekend with Marcus St. James? You better believe I was going to look the best I possibly could. I was on a mission, and that mission was to make this man fall at my feet.

I quickly brushed my teeth and fixed my hair, and my eyes caught on the pristine white tiles of the shower behind me. Again, I thought what a damn shame it was that Marcus had declined my invitation to share it last night. The thing was enormous and had so many shower heads it looked like a carwash. After standing under it for a good ten minutes, I could also report that it definitely cleaned you…everywhere.

I headed back to the bedroom, where I grabbed some jeans and a light knit sweater. I had no idea what I was going to be doing today. It was Saturday, but if I knew Marcus at all, that didn't mean he was having a break.

The news didn't stop just because it was the weekend and he *was* the news. Or at least the head of it. So I wondered how he spent his weekends. One thing I did know for certain: he'd promised to show me something he liked to do for fun, and I was going to hold him to that.

Hell, maybe I could convince him to start now. I tossed

my clothes back on the bed and grinned, opting for just the robe, then I headed for the door to go and track him down.

When I stepped out into the hall, it was the first time I got to really look around by myself. I'd seen it last night, of course, but my mind was in a foggy dream state and, well, Marcus had been there. Whenever he was near, it was hard to concentrate on anything other than him—but this place was extraordinary.

It was full of rich, luxurious textures, from the woods, to the marble, to the drapery and fabrics. It was simply spectacular.

Original wooden floors stretched the length of the hall, and the sumptuous red oak paneling from downstairs also lined the walls up here. It was like walking through a museum, it was so well preserved. When I reached the main staircase with a banister wide enough for me to slide down, I took in the art hanging from the walls as I slowly headed down to the ground level.

I looked toward the office where one of the best nights of my life had taken place, but when I noticed it was empty, I headed in the opposite direction. I still couldn't get over the fact that with a house this size, Marcus didn't have a butler or personal chef milling about. But then again, it wasn't that much of a surprise. One of the first things I'd noticed about him was how much he enjoyed his solitude. So it made sense that he preferred his house to remain his own private sanctuary, and the fact that I had been invited inside wasn't lost on me.

I tightened the belt of my robe and kept on moving

through the halls, and then the distinct sound of music playing caught my attention. I headed in that direction, and as I got closer, the music got louder, and I recognized the song in an instant. "Moon River" by Andy Williams.

Something about the fact that this was the song Marcus was listening to on a Saturday morning made me smile. I stepped into the kitchen and found him standing at the counter reading the morning paper.

In black sweatpants and a white t-shirt, this was the first time I'd ever seen him look so...relaxed. He had a mug in one hand and his phone in the other, as he took a sip of what I presumed was the delicious coffee I could smell in the air.

Directly in front of him was a set of double doors that led out to a private deck that had a table set up for eating and couches amongst bursts of greenery and colorful flowers. It was so charming and unexpected that you almost forgot you were in the middle of the city, except for the glimpse of the mammoth high-rise building through the branches just beyond.

As the song ended, Marcus must've caught the sound of my feet on his tiled floor. He glanced over his shoulder, and the second his eyes locked on mine, I could barely stay upright.

With his beard neatly trimmed and his hair a little messy from a quick hand through the longer strands, he was one hell of a thing to wake up to, and I could only imagine how it would feel to do that in his bed.

"Good morning."

Jesus. That gravelly voice made my heart beat a little

faster as Marcus put his phone down, then turned and leaned against the counter.

"Good morning."

He took a sip of his coffee. "Did you sleep well?"

"Best night's sleep I've had in a long time."

"I'm glad to hear it. You look"—his gaze drifted down to the white robe where it gaped open at my chest—"well rested."

"I am, thanks. I had to get a good night's sleep. It's been a busy week, and I have this very demanding boss who doesn't even give me the weekends off."

"What a tyrant."

"Total tyrant."

"Huh. Well, maybe if you ask him nicely, he'll make you a cup of coffee to help get you through the day."

I sidled in a little closer to him, and Marcus pushed off the counter to stand up straight. It seemed he was trying to keep some distance between us this morning, but that wasn't going to work for me.

I reached for his coffee mug and looked at the contents, pulling a face. "Please tell me you have milk and sugar?"

"I do, if that's what you'd like."

"It is. I'll take two sugars, please," I said, and then gave his mug back. "I need it to keep me sweet."

Marcus scoffed and moved over to his espresso machine, so I hitched myself up onto his counter and watched him work.

"So, what's on the agenda today, boss?"

Marcus arched a brow then went back to what he was doing. "I have some work to do—"

"Naturally. But then? Something *fun*, right? That was the deal."

Marcus grabbed a small silver jug out of the cupboard and poured some milk into it. "I know the deal. I actually had something planned already. I'm just waiting to make sure I can be accommodated before committing to it. But I don't believe it will be a problem."

I narrowed my eyes. "Could you be more cryptic?"

"I could be. In fact, I need you to go with Franklin today and pick up something in case it all turns out."

"You're not going to tell me what I'm picking up, are you?"

"No."

"That's mean."

Marcus shrugged as he began to froth the milk. "That's who I am. You better get used to it."

I didn't believe that for a second. Yes, Marcus was serious ninety-eight percent of the time, and sported a perpetual frown. But the other two percent, he was sexy, sarcastic, and nearly damn perfect, if you asked me.

"Fine. I'll go where I'm told, but you better have a backup if this original plan falls through."

"It won't."

"He says with such authority."

Marcus picked up the coffee cup and handed it over to me. He'd made a perfect cappuccino, with the chocolate powder on top and everything.

"Is there anyone who doesn't do what you tell them to do?"

"You," he said as he tapped me on the leg and gestured to his paper.

I glanced down at the paper and then back to him and grinned. "That's not true. I did everything you told me to do last night."

"You only did that because it got you what you wanted."

True. But I did it just the same. That should count for something, right?

Marcus took my chin in a firm grip. "I like that you stand up to me," he said, and let me go. "It's one of the reasons I followed you out of the conference room that night."

"*One* of them?" I scooted off the counter. "How many are there?"

Marcus grabbed his paper and tucked it under his arm before reaching for his previously abandoned coffee. "Enough that I'm leaving before your hands are free again."

I laughed. "Worried I'll put them on you?"

He shook his head as he backed out of the kitchen. "Worried you won't, and I have work to do. There's food in the fridge—help yourself—and Franklin will be here in a few hours to pick you up. I'll see you later, Gabe."

CHAPTER 23

MARCUS

IT WAS LATE afternoon as I sat in my office and finished up what felt like the millionth call today regarding the downfall of Brian Evans. He'd made a monumentally bad decision last week on air, live, for everyone to see, and walking it back was proving damn near impossible.

That was one of the true tests that came with being an on-air journalist in today's industry. You had to present facts on both sides of the aisle in an unbiased way, and if you were in any way overly opinionated and *wrong*, then shit would hit the fan—and in Brian's case, he now stank.

No one wanted to touch him with a ten-foot pole. His ratings had plummeted overnight, and the opposition stations were having a field day with it. Gloria wanted him out, I'd relayed that crystal clear, and though I agreed that that was the quick solution, Brian was a damn good journalist beneath his current frustrations, and I'd somehow managed to convince the network to send him on an extended hiatus.

We'd let the dust settle and temperatures in the room cool, and then maybe we could revisit the situation.

I let out a sigh and a ran hand through my hair. It was moments like this that I wished I had a simple nine-to-five Monday-through-Friday job. But in all honesty, I'd likely end up wanting to pull my hair out.

I wasn't good at sitting still. I just wasn't built that way. Fun was something I did on occasion, and once it was over, I was ready to get back to work. Most didn't understand that drive, but it was an innate part of me, something that would never go away and could only be worked around.

I closed my eyes for a second and thought about what I had planned for the evening, and wondered what Gabe's reaction would be. A night at the symphony wasn't exactly for everyone. Sean had reminded me of the time I'd given him and Alexander tickets to join me, so I couldn't begin to imagine how a young man like Gabe would react.

One thing I did know: it'd been nice to see him standing in my kitchen this morning in nothing more than a robe—*too* nice. He'd looked comfortable, like he belonged, and he was the first man I'd wanted to see there over and over again.

My phone rang, and when I saw who was calling, a smile lit my face. I hit *accept* and brought it to my ear.

"Hello there, Miss Abby."

"Hey, hey Marcus," my younger sister Abigail said with a smile in her voice. "How are you on this lovely Saturday evening? Relaxed, I hope."

I glanced out the window at the twinkling lights in the courtyard. "I'm getting there."

"Getting there? That doesn't count. It's such a beautiful night. You should be out in it."

"I will get out in it. I was just finishing up with some work when you called."

"Work, schmerk," she said, and I could nearly see her roll her eyes. "It's Saturday."

"I'm aware. I actually have plans to go out tonight."

"Oh *reeeally*? And where are you going? And who are you going with?" she said, nosey as ever. She was a romance writer, and a perpetual matchmaker who believed that everyone had a soul mate. She'd dedicated far too many hours to finding mine. "If you say yourself, Marcus, don't think I won't come over there and smack you in the head."

I chuckled, because she wasn't lying. Abigail was eight years my junior—a surprise baby whom I more or less raised due to busy parents—and the first thing I'd made sure she knew how to do was stand up for herself, both physically and mentally.

We had a close relationship, one I cherished above all others, but I knew I needed to work on that or risk turning into the strangers my parents had become to us.

"There is nothing wrong with enjoying your own company."

"Ugh, that's just sad."

"Tonight, however, I am going out with a—"

"Don't say friend. That's almost as bad as saying alone."

"I can't say *anything* with you constantly interrupting

me." I heard a sound at my office door and looked up to see Gabe standing in the doorway.

He had his right arm bent so the two garment bags hooked over his index finger rested over his shoulder, and he was leaning against the frame as though he didn't have a care in the world.

I leaned back in my chair and let my gaze sweep down over his light grey knit sweater and tight blue jeans. "He's not a...friend, per se."

Gabe arched an eyebrow. I crooked my finger for him to enter, and he did as he was told.

"What does that mean?" Abigail asked.

I smiled. "Exactly what I said."

"You didn't say anything."

"That's not true. I spoke."

"And said nothing. Just some cryptic answer that— Ooh, is he there?"

When Gabe came to a standstill, I had a flash of the way he'd looked naked in this room the night before. "That would be correct."

"Oh my God. So he really *isn't* a friend. Is he...more?"

I could tell Abigail was coming up with all different kinds of scenarios in that rose-colored world she lived in. But I wasn't about to tell her that I'd blackmailed Gabe into being my errand boy for a week after he lied to me about who he was during our one-night stand.

So I ignored the question altogether. "I need to go."

"Of course you do. Go, *go*— Oh, wait. I have a book launch this week—Wednesday. You have to come."

"Abby, you know I hate those big parties—"

"Please, Marcus. Come on. You could bring your 'friend.'"

Hmm, that wasn't such a bad idea, and at least with Gabe there I wouldn't be bored out of my mind.

"Okay, send me over the details."

"Ah! Fantastic. And don't think I won't be asking about all of this the next time we talk."

Of that I had no doubt. But at least I could come up with something more appropriate for her by then. "I look forward to it."

"Have a good night," she said with an air of excitement, and her enthusiasm was contagious.

"I will. I'll talk to you soon. Love you." Gabe's eyes widened, and I smirked as I ended the call. "Welcome back."

"Thanks." He shifted the bags off his shoulder and held them up in front of him. "Two tuxedos. I believe that is what was on order. At least, that's what the old guy in the tailor shop said. By the way, I didn't even know they had those anymore."

"Tailor shops?"

"Yes. With little old men who have a tape measure draped around their neck."

I nodded and got to my feet, and then walked around the desk to take the items from him.

"Who's Abby?"

His curiosity at what he'd overheard was clearly too much for him to ignore. "My sister."

"You have a sister?"

"I do."

"Weird. I totally figured you for an only child."

"Oh? And why is that?"

"Because you always get what you want. I figured that rolled over from childhood."

I eyed him and shook my head, before reading the tags on the hangers and handing one back to him.

Gabe looked at the garment bag and frowned. "Did you need me to take this one back?"

"No. I need you to go and shower and then put it on. You're going to need that for where we're going tonight."

"Excuse me?" Gabe laughed and then looked at the bag again.

"You asked me to show you something I do for fun. Luckily, my request from earlier was met."

"Was there ever any doubt?"

"Not really, no."

"And I need to wear a tux?"

"Yes." I draped mine over my arm as he slowly unzipped the bag a couple inches and looked inside.

"What *fun* thing could you possibly do that needs a tux? Oh God, it's not someone's wedding, is it?"

I chuckled at his mortified expression. "Do you have something against the institution?"

"No, but the idea of sitting through some stranger's wedding ceremony and then all those boring speeches—"

"It's not a wedding, Gabe. Plus, I said it's something I do for fun. That's hardly an activity that I can do often."

He eyed me carefully, and I could see the wheels turning. "And I *have* to wear a tux?"

"You don't have to, but it's encouraged."

He looked back to the bag and re-zipped it, then studied the tag at the top. "Wait, how did you know my exact measurements?"

I didn't. I'd taken a guess. But that guess had been backed up by some pretty solid research. "I've been watching you very closely for the past few days, and last night, I took a nice, long look."

Gabe stepped toward me, and I curled my fingers into the bag to make sure I didn't grab him.

"That's really hot."

So was he, and I knew he was going to look stunning in that tuxedo tonight.

"So is this like...a date?"

The twinkle in his eyes told me he knew exactly what my answer would be, but he was willing to push the issue anyway. It was clear Gabe wanted something more here, but realistically, that wasn't going to happen.

"No. This is me fulfilling your request. I don't have time to date."

"But if you did, would this be a date?"

I shook my head. "No."

"Why not?"

Jesus, he was persistent when it came to going after something he wanted. I knew that from the night of the work party. He kept at it until he had his answer or his prize, and this would be no different.

"You're too young, I'm too busy, and we have nothing in common."

"I know one thing we have in common."

"Gabe..."

"What? I was going to say Mitchell & Madison. We have that in common." The twitch of his lips exposed his comment for the lie it was, but I wasn't about to get into this with him now. If we went down the path of the one thing we truly had in common, we wouldn't get to our final destination of the evening.

He sighed when I remained silent. "Okay, be stubborn. What time should I be ready for you tonight, Mr. St. James?"

Something about the way he said that made my cock throb in time with my now-thumping heart. "Seven?"

"Seven it is." He walked back toward my office door, but before he disappeared, he said, "By the way, I hope you don't mind that at least for tonight, I'm going to be thinking of this as a date."

I opened my mouth to respond, but before I could get anything out, the charming flirt had disappeared out the door.

CHAPTER 24
GABE

"WHY WON'T YOU tell me where we're going?" I said for the tenth time in the span of five minutes. But ever since we'd climbed in the back of Marcus's SUV, Marcus hadn't said a word—not one. Here we were dressed in tuxedos, for God's sake, and he was being all closed-lipped about it.

Deciding to try a different tactic, I leaned forward and said over Franklin's shoulder, "Do you know where we're going tonight?"

Franklin looked in the rearview mirror but said nothing, so I tried the next best thing—guessing.

"An award ceremony."

Marcus eyed me and shook his head. "No."

Well, at least he was talking now. Okay, where else could we be going? He'd said it was fun. What would Marcus consider fun?

Oh no... "Is it another work party?"

He frowned. "No. But it's good to know how much fun you had at the last one."

"I had...fun."

"Yes, I can tell by the expression on your face."

"I did." I lowered my eyes to his lap and licked my lips. "I had a lot fun on the *studio tour* I took. Does that count?"

Marcus's lips curved. "Yes, I believe it does."

"See, I told you. So are you taking me somewhere we can have *that* kind of fun again? Oh—" I pretended to look shocked. "Is that a fantasy of yours? To be caught in public doing something risqué?"

Marcus let out a bark of laughter, and the sound was so rare that I took a second to revel in it. "Definitely not."

"Well that's a shame."

"I have to say, I agree. However, you told me you wanted to know something *I* do for fun."

"I *know*. So will you just put me out of my misery?" Just as those words left my mouth, Franklin came to a stop outside of a red brick building with the names Bach, Mozart, Beethoven, Schubert, and Wagner inscribed above five large windows, and I could hardly believe my eyes.

We had just stopped outside of— "The Orchestra Hall at the Symphony Center?"

I'd been so caught up in trying to guess what Marcus had planned that I hadn't been paying attention to where Franklin was driving us. But I knew exactly where we were now, and I also knew why.

"We're going to the symphony?"

Marcus looked out the window to all the people elegantly dressed for a night of classical music.

"That's right," he said, and turned back to face me.

I tried to make sense of this, tried to work out if I'd let something slip when we'd been together, or—

"Have you ever been before?"

—it was just some cosmic twist of fate, and that right there was my answer.

I hadn't slipped up anywhere. This is what *he* did for fun, and I couldn't have been happier to learn that little piece of information. So much for having nothing in common.

"I have been before, yes."

"Let me guess, you hated it."

"No, um..." I tried to school my features so I wouldn't start laughing. But really, this was too much. "I love classical music."

Marcus didn't look convinced. "Are you just saying that because you're about to sit through two hours of it?"

A wide smile crossed my lips, and this time I let a laugh free. But if he was going to be cryptic and cagey tonight, well, so was I. "I guess you won't find out until you take me in there, will you?"

He inclined his head, and as Franklin went to get out, Marcus said, "I've got it tonight, Franklin."

"Very well, Mr. St. James."

Marcus turned back to me. "Wait for me here."

He climbed out of the Escalade, and when he shut the door I looked to Franklin in the rearview mirror and saw his eyes crinkle at the sides, as though he were smiling. But before I could ask him what about, the door was open and Marcus stood in front of me looking like some dashing blond prince.

For a second all I could do was sit there and stare, because I'd never been so captivated in my life. When he held his hand out to me, I found myself wishing that this night would never end.

Marcus was everything I'd ever dreamed of whenever I'd thought about who I could see myself falling for, and this moment was like some added fairy magic that had been sprinkled on top.

"Are you ready?"

I would've said yes whether I was ready or not, just so I could touch him again. I slipped my hand into his and climbed out of the SUV. I glanced up at the red brick facade of Orchestra Hall and thought it had never looked more beautiful than it did tonight, with the floodlights illuminating each of the names etched into the stone.

"Is everything okay?" Marcus asked.

I nodded. "Everything is perfect. Absolutely perfect."

A curious light entered Marcus's eyes, and then he half smiled. "Good. Then let's head inside so we can find our seats."

He didn't have to tell me twice. Marcus led me toward the front entrance and through the beautifully restored lobby, where we headed up stairs to the second floor and over toward the east entrance.

As we approached the lady by the door collecting tickets, Marcus reached inside his jacket and produced two, and then it clicked.

"That's what you were trying to get this morning."

We stopped behind several other patrons waiting to be ushered inside, and Marcus looked down at me. "Hmm?"

"An extra ticket. You said you were waiting to see if you could be accommodated."

So this really was what Marcus had planned to do tonight, and that couldn't have worked out more perfectly for me than if I had picked it myself.

"That's right. I had one ticket already and luckily was able to secure a second at the last minute."

"Just like that?"

"No, not *just* like that. It took several phone calls and persuasive discussions."

Okay, something about that was extremely sexy. Marcus had somehow managed to talk his way into getting an extra seat beside him at the sold-out symphony—for me. I had no doubt the performance had been booked solid. It was a Saturday night, and these die-hard fans held season tickets, so I wondered how exactly he'd gone about getting someone to give up their place.

As we stepped up to the lady, her face lit up in a brilliant smile. "Good evening, Mr. St. James."

"Good evening, Tanya. It's lovely to see you."

"And you too, of course. As always, we're thrilled to have you here with us, and your seats are ready, just as requested."

"Thank you. I appreciate that."

Her eyes shifted to me, and she held out a program. "This will tell you who is playing tonight and what instrument. You have two of the best seats in the house. I'm slightly jealous."

I couldn't stop my smile as I took the program from her. "Thank you. I kind of have to pinch myself too."

She laughed and gestured inside the doors with her small flashlight. "Straight ahead and to your left."

Marcus gave a clipped nod before leading me inside the hall, and when the red velvet chairs and brightly lit stage came into view, I stopped for a minute and caught my breath. My fingers tightened around Marcus's as I stared down at the chairs neatly positioned in their usual semicircle. The conductor's podium was front and center, and off to the back left was the piano and harp. To the right of that, the percussion was set up, and as more patrons began to enter the hall, Marcus leaned down and said by my ear, "Are you sure everything's okay?"

I turned until we were practically nose to nose and felt a little giddy with the excitement thrumming through me. "Yes. Everything's fantastic. Seriously, I'm just taking it all in."

Marcus eyed me closely, as though trying to see beneath the words I was saying. "I thought you said you'd been before."

"I have, but not for a while."

He nodded and then gestured for us to keep walking. "Then let's take our seats so we can enjoy it."

I aimed a brilliant smile at him, and lo and behold, he returned it.

My stomach did a weird kind of flip that had nothing to do with nerves, excitement, or sex, but everything to do with a new emotion that was coursing through me. But I wasn't going to let the moment overwhelm me. I wasn't going to let it confuse me. So I tucked that feeling away to examine later and followed Marcus to our waiting seats.

When he reached the first row of chairs lining the balcony, I could barely contain myself, knowing we were going to have a first-class view. But then he made a left, headed around a partition, and holy shit, we were in a box seat.

My mouth fell open as my feet came to a dead stop and I spotted two seats overlooking the balcony with a table between them and—no way—two dirty martinis.

"After you," Marcus said by my ear, and gestured to the seats.

I tried to send a message from my brain to my feet to move, but it was still too busy trying to process what it was seeing.

When I'd issued the little amendment to our deal about having fun, I'd expected a movie or board games, something plain and simple. But no matter what Marcus wanted to believe, *this* was a date.

Not only had he gone out of his way to secure a private place for us to enjoy the show, he'd rented me a tuxedo and had the drinks we first shared together ready and waiting for us.

The fact that that he enjoyed something that was so near and dear to my own heart was something he didn't even realize yet. But he would by the end of this evening, because unbeknownst to him, Marcus St. James had just brought me home.

CHAPTER 25

MARCUS

THE SYMPHONY HAD always been the one place in the world that I could escape to. The lights would dim, then go dark, and everyone in the world faded away as music took over.

Tonight, however, something else had captured my attention—or should I say someone else. We were nearing the end of the evening, well into the second set, and I couldn't have told you one piece that had been played, too caught up was I in the beautiful man seated beside me.

From the moment we arrived tonight at Orchestra Hall, something had changed in Gabe. There was a certain *je ne sais quoi* that I couldn't quite put my finger on. But he seemed right at home here, in a place where I'd expected him to feel like a fish out of water.

I could count on one hand the people I'd met who appreciated the fine arts with the kind of maturity he'd displayed tonight. But the wonder in his eyes and attention he'd paid to the musicians below almost made me a little jealous. He was entranced, spellbound by the magic created on stage, and tonight, I was enchanted by him.

Dressed to impress in the tuxedo I'd rented for him, Gabe looked even more handsome than usual. The crisp white shirt against his delicious complexion drew the eye to his angular jaw and high cheeks. The jacket and pants fit him as though they'd been made specifically for him, and instead of looking uncomfortable in any way, he wore the outfit with a certain finesse that not many could pull off.

He was watching the performance with such concentration it was as though he were memorizing it. Unable to keep away from him any longer, I leaned over to him. "Are you enjoying yourself?"

Gabe turned to look at me, and no words were needed. The color on his cheeks and excitement in his eyes were answer enough. He looked like a kid in a candy store.

"So much. You don't know how much I needed this."

That was an odd choice of words, but before I could ask him to elaborate, he returned his attention to the performance below.

I settled back in my seat, continued to study him, and tried to work out what was happening here. This was more than someone who merely enjoyed the musical arts. He was fully invested, one hundred percent immersed in what he was experiencing, and when the final movement was over, and everyone stood to give a well-deserved ovation, Gabe turned to me with a look of pure, unadulterated joy in his eyes.

"Oh my God. That was amazing." His smile lit up the shadows we were standing in.

"I agree. They were wonderful tonight."

"They're wonderful every night."

There he went again, saying things that didn't quite seem to fit what I knew of him, and yet tonight, they somehow did.

"I'm so pleased you enjoyed yourself. This is one of my favorite things to do, go to the symphony."

"Oh, me too." Gabe glanced back to the stage where the musicians were now talking among themselves as they went about packing up their instruments, and if I didn't know better, I could've sworn I felt a sense of longing from him.

"Would you like to go down there?"

Gabe whirled around and looked almost guilty. As though I'd caught him with his hand in the cookie jar.

"I... Is that something we can do?"

"Definitely." I held out my hand, the need to touch him now stronger than ever before. "I'm a frequent patron here, and also one of the donors."

"One of?" he asked, angling his head to look me in the eye. "Or the biggest?"

"I'm generous with the things I enjoy. I'm sure others are too."

Gabe grinned. "Mhmm. You somehow managed to get a spare ticket to a sold-out performance in a *box* seat. You must be *very* generous."

The dimples winking at me were worth the fun he was poking, so I let it slide. "Would you like to go down there or not?"

He nodded. "I would love to."

"Then let's go."

We walked out of the seating area, and when we reached the doors, I spotted Tanya. I got her attention, and within minutes we were being led downstairs. Gabe's hand was all but strangling mine, and it was like he was about to meet the Queen.

We entered the lower floor as everyone else was exiting. Gabe's excitement vibrated off him. As Tanya headed up the stairs to where the conductor stood chatting with one of the musicians, I was about to tell Gabe to relax when I heard, *"Gabriel?"*

Wait, did they just say—

"Gabriel Romero?"

Yes, one of the men on stage holding a violin had definitely just said his name. I came to an abrupt halt and turned to look at Gabe.

He shrugged and gave me a cheeky grin. "Surprise."

Surprise? What was he talking about? Before I could ask him, though, Gabe let go of my hand and headed toward the stage, and my confusion doubled.

"I knew it was you. We haven't seen you around here in forever," the man said as Gabe walked over to the steps and, casual as you please, went up onto the stage.

It wasn't often that I was caught off guard, but when

Gabe headed across the stage and *several* members greeted him, I was completely thrown off.

What the hell was going on?

"I know," Gabe said to the man with the violin. "But after everything that happened, I needed some time."

"That's understandable. God, I'd feel the same way."

When Gabe was close enough, the two of them embraced. "You guys were phenomenal tonight," he said, then peered around Mr. Violin to look down at me. "Weren't they, Marcus?"

I narrowed my eyes, still having zero idea what was going on. "Yes. The performance was one of the best I've seen."

In all fairness, that might've had to do with the fact that I'd enjoyed it through Gabe's eyes, and he clearly had a strong connection to the music *and* these people.

"See," Gabe said. "And he's your biggest fan. That's some high praise right there."

They all accepted the compliment with grace, and then a petite lady with pin-straight, shoulder-length black hair walked out on stage and froze.

"*Gabe?*"

Gabe glanced in her direction, and she ran across the stage to embrace him. I recognized her from the second tier of the stage—she'd been playing one of the cellos—and when they finally let go of one another, she said something that just about knocked me off my feet.

"Are you still playing?"

Playing? As in an instrument? No. There was no way

Gabe played a musical instrument and I didn't know about it.

But how would I know? It wasn't as though I'd taken the time to really get to know him beyond the physical, and suddenly I felt like the biggest asshole around.

Gabe grimaced as he slipped his hands into his pockets and shrugged. "Well, I was told I have to keep playing to keep sharp, you know? But it's been slow going. After the accident I had weeks of rest and then therapy, so I'm pretty rusty."

"Oh, come on." She reached out to squeeze his shoulder. "Even rusty, I bet you still run circles around me."

Gabe was in an accident? What kind of accident? And how badly had he been hurt? Then the woman's words began to repeat in my head. He could *run circles around her?*

My eyes shifted to the cello. Did that mean he played? Had I seen him play up there on that stage and not even known it? So many questions were running through my head.

"I promise you, I can't," Gabe said, interrupting my thoughts.

"Prove it," she said with a laugh, and I wanted to echo her. If what I was now thinking was true, I wanted Gabe to prove it too.

"What? No." Gabe shook his head. "I'm here tonight as a guest, in case you missed it."

With a sassy hand on her hip, the young lady held her

bow out to him, and before Gabe had a chance to refuse, I decided to put in my own two cents.

"I want to see." Everyone on the stage turned in my direction. But my eyes were locked on only one man, and when Gabe stepped around his friend and those luminous eyes met mine, I added, "Play for me."

CHAPTER 26

GABE

PLAY FOR HIM? With the way Marcus was looking at me, I was positive I would do *anything* for him.

All night he seemed somewhat worried over whether I'd be bored in coming here. But now that he knew the truth and his concern had been replaced with fascination—call me arrogant, but I suddenly wanted to show off for him.

"Come on, Gabe," Dominique said. "I haven't heard you play in months."

That was true. She'd been in the year above me at Northwestern and was a graduate now. Last year we'd both been offered a place in the symphony upon our graduation, and that marked a milestone, as I was the youngest to ever be chosen. After my accident, however, everything had changed. Dominique had become the youngest, and I'd had to walk away from my dream—for the time being.

"Okay, I'll play. But it's been a while, so don't judge me."

"Oh, come on. You were always the better of the two of

us. You could hear a song once and then play it by ear. Don't start acting modest now."

I looked over to see Dominique's cello resting on its stand and took in a fortifying breath. I hadn't played in public for months, and to do it now in front of Marcus was slightly intimidating. But I could feel the adrenaline beginning to hum through my veins now and knew that nothing was going to stop me.

"Gabe?"

I looked over to see Marcus walking toward the stage. As he drew closer, I found my feet moving, and by the time he reached me, that low hum had turned into a full-on adrenaline rush.

"Play something for me. I want to watch."

Damn, there was no way I was saying no to that. The idea of him standing in the audience watching me perform just for him was too irresistible to refuse.

I swallowed and nodded, and only hoped my efforts beyond the walls of the university had kept my skill level even a tenth of what it had once been. "Do you have any requests?"

His smile was slow and sensual and unlike any he'd graced me with before, and my heart thumped fast.

"Why don't you pick something for me that you think I'd enjoy?"

I licked my lips. Jesus, I needed to get away from him before I threw myself off the stage and into his arms. "I think I can come up with something."

As I straightened, Marcus took a step back and slipped

his hands into his pockets, and holy hell, he looked phenomenal there under the hall's main lights.

"Of that I have no doubt."

I nodded and turned to Dominique. "Are you sure you don't mind if I—"

"Stop. You know I don't." She swept her hand toward her instrument, and I made my way to the seat behind it.

As I settled down and brought the cello between my splayed thighs, all I could think about was the way I'd stood naked between Marcus's the night before. I shifted on the seat, knowing that thoughts like that would do nothing but distract me, and positioned the instrument so its weight was supported on its endpin, and the lower bout was steadied between my knees. I rested the upper bout against my chest and the neck against my shoulder, and as I sat there getting a feel for the instrument, I thought that at least I had a rhythm to play to with the steady beating of my heart.

Several members from tonight's performance stopped what they were doing to look at me as I racked my brain on what to play. There were so many possibilities, both classical and contemporary, but when I looked over to Marcus, everything but him faded from view, and my only goal was to impress him. I had the exact song.

I closed my eyes and thought of the song, the melody inside my head, and as the famous tune composed by Henry Mancini began to take form, I started to play.

I plucked at the strings to give myself a bass line, then I brought the bow up and let the music take me over, the strings vibrating beneath my fingertips as the beautiful and yearning tune filled the hall.

With the instrument still mic'ed up, the calm, melodic tone swept me away as I sank into the wondrous feeling of being caught up in another world. I imagined the lyrics with every sweep of my bow, "Moon River" coming to life all around me—the idea of being carried off somewhere new *by* someone new, the exact message I wanted to send to Marcus in this moment, because that was what he was doing to me.

As the honesty in the lyrics began to hit home, I opened my eyes and noticed he had moved to my side of the stage. He was watching me like a man in a trance, and there was a look of complete wonder swirling in those blue eyes.

My heart swelled as my body filled with pride, and as I launched into the second verse, that slow smile from earlier curved his lips, and the power just about knocked me off my seat.

When the song ended and everyone began to clap, the only person I was interested in walked up onto the stage. I placed the bow down and set the instrument back in its stand, and by the time Marcus reached me, I was on my feet.

I was about to ask him what he thought, but before I could say a word, his hands were in my hair and his lips were on my mouth. He was kissing every thought right out of my mind, and as the stage began to spin and the lights began to blur, I had to grip the lapels of his jacket to stay upright.

When he finally raised his head, there was a fierce look of desire, and that made me feel like I was flying.

"That was..." Marcus rested his forehead against mine. "I'm speechless."

I grinned, rather proud of myself. "Is that a first?"

"It just might be."

"Then I'll take it as a compliment."

"You should. Jesus, Gabe. You're extraordinary."

I chuckled and shook my head. "I'm rusty."

Marcus took my hands and looked at the scars there. But before he could say anything else, Dominique came up beside us with a huge grin on her face.

"I see no rust." She looked to Marcus. "Do you see any rust?"

"No. All I see is gold."

The fact that he was looking in my eyes when he said that made goosebumps break out across my skin. All I wanted right then was to get the hell out of there and go somewhere private with him.

"You listen to me, Mr. Romero," Dominique said, pointing a finger at me. "The second you can get back and finish that degree, do it. You owe yourself. Hell, you owe the whole world. You can't let a talent like that go to waste."

I could still feel Marcus's attention on me, but, not wanting to get into all of that right now, I quickly brushed the subject aside.

"I will. But enough about that and me. *You* were all excellent tonight. Thanks for letting me pretend up here for a minute."

"It shouldn't be pretend," she said. "But you're welcome anytime."

"Thanks." I waved to everyone else, then turned to Marcus, who was looking at me as though we'd just met, and in a way, we had. He'd never been introduced to Gabriel Romero the university student and musician, and I'd gotten really good at forgetting that guy existed, because this past week I'd found something else to occupy my time—him.

"Are you ready to go?" That sexy voice made a shiver of pleasure race down my spine. As his warm fingers engulfed mine, every nerve ending in my body came to life. I could feel the air around us sizzling with tension as he guided us out of the hall and into the crisp night air.

Franklin was front and center waiting for us, just as I'd suspected he would be, and when he opened the SUV's door and I had to let go of Marcus's hand, I was disappointed until he climbed in behind me.

He pulled the door shut, and Franklin remained standing guard outside, and it didn't take a genius to realize that Marcus had just asked for some privacy.

"That was quite the surprise in there tonight. *You* were quite the surprise."

I turned in the seat so I was facing him then reached out to run a finger down his sleeve. "A good surprise?"

"The best I've ever had."

"Oh." I grinned. "So now I have to top myself?"

Marcus shook his head. "If you think for one second I'm falling for that, you're mistaken."

"Falling for what?"

He captured my wandering hand and stilled it. "The sneaky little innuendo you just slipped in there."

"I was just making an observation. It's not my fault you have a dirty mind."

"It's one hundred percent your fault, and you know it. From the minute I met you, I haven't been able to get you off my mind. And what you played in there tonight, I'll never stop hearing. These fingers are magic. They cast spells."

He brought my hand to his mouth and kissed my fingertips, and I sighed.

"And what spell have they cast over you?"

Marcus studied me closely. "Damned if I know, but I don't want it to end here."

I reached out and ran my fingers through his hair, then said against his lips, "Take me home."

"Be sure."

"I've always been sure."

"And understand that this has nothing to do with our deal."

That was the last thing on my mind. I kissed my way along his jaw to his ear and whispered, "As long as you understand that it never did."

CHAPTER 27

MARCUS

WHEN WE ARRIVED at the house and climbed out of the car, no words were spoken as we made our way inside.

So many things had happened tonight, so many things I wanted to know more about. But when I placed my hands on the door by his head, all of that disappeared and all that remained was the two of us.

"I really should say goodnight now, and go and do some work."

Gabe nodded as he stared up at me from beneath his thick lashes. "Okay. But before you go, let me say thank you and goodnight." He slid his hand over my shoulder to the back of my neck, then gently pulled my head down and brushed his mouth over the top of mine.

His lips were soft and warm and so damn tempting that there was no hope of stopping my groan of pleasure. He was like a dream, an illusion I'd created to fill a part of my life that I hadn't realized was so empty. When he pulled back, I took his chin and stared into his eyes.

"I said I should, not that I was going to."

His smile made it impossible not to take another taste, and without another word, I guided us upstairs. As we passed by his room, Gabe's fingers tightened around mine, and for a second I wondered if he would put a stop to this. After all, *he'd* made the rules about not sleeping together during this arrangement. I'd just been trying my best to uphold them.

I was done with that, though. If he wanted this to stop then he was the one who had to do so. My control was gone, my power to resist what I so desperately wanted nowhere in sight. When we reached the door to my room, I stopped and turned to him.

"I want you in my bed tonight."

That flirty smirk that was so inherently Gabe appeared, and my pulse skyrocketed.

"Then take me there."

Any thought that he might be unsure about this was quickly dismissed, and I pushed down on the handle and opened the door. I watched him walk in ahead of me and reluctantly let him go.

Oval in shape, my bedroom was on the side of the home that housed the always-talked-about turret. Gabe walked across the hardwood floors to the rug that the bed sat on. He stopped and looked up at the high-peaked roof, and his eyes widened at the chandelier that hung over the bed.

Other than that, the room was fairly minimalistic,

considering the size and space. The only furniture in here apart from the bed and nightstands was a dresser and a loveseat. The colors were creams and golds to match the warm glow of the chandelier. Gabe came to a stop at the end of the bed and pushed his fingers into the plush covers, and my cock stiffened in response.

I'd dreamed of this moment back when I hadn't even known his name. I'd lain in the bed he was now standing beside and imagined him in it with me. By the end of this night, that dream would finally be a reality.

"Hmm, so soft."

"Not exactly the word that's coming to my mind right now."

"No?" Gabe grinned as I closed the door behind me. "You're right. The word that comes to mind whenever I think about you is...sexy."

I unbuttoned my jacket and crossed the room.

Gabe lowered his gaze over me. "So damn sexy. And us together? We're hot as hell. Admit it."

I scoffed at his arrogance and tossed my jacket over the end of the mattress, then I reached for my bow tie and tugged it free. As I unbuttoned my shirt and the material parted, a low groan left Gabe, and one of his hands moved under his jacket.

"Gabe?" I said. His eyes immediately found mine. "Get rid of the jacket. I want to see those magic hands of yours."

He grinned like a fiend and immediately flicked the buttons free, then he dropped his jacket on the floor, revealing the clear outline of his erection under the tight fit of his pants.

"Fuck," I said, and drew down my zipper.

Gabe reached down and massaged the hard-on hidden behind the expensive black fabric. "Admit it," he said again. "Admit how hot we are together. We all but set that studio on fire that night. God, I can't tell you how many times I've gotten off to that."

I hooked my fingers inside his pants and tugged him forward until his shoes met mine. "Instead of telling you, how about I show you instead."

I crushed my lips against his in a kiss full of want and desire, and when he moved to his toes and angled his head, allowing deeper access, I attacked. I thrust my tongue between his lips and tangled it with his.

He was delicious, and so fucking eager, as he reached for the back of my neck. I grabbed a handful of his ass and ground my erection alongside his as he bit and sucked at my lips like he'd never get enough.

"Marcus," he said.

"Are you getting hotter?"

"Fuck yes."

"Good, because so am I."

I loosened my hold on him and took a step back. Gabe tugged on his bow tie and said, "Then maybe you should take your clothes off."

Bold to the very end, that was Gabe, and that turned me on even more. "In a hurry, are we?"

He shrugged out of his shirt and dropped it on the floor. "What do you think?"

"I think you need to get on my bed in the next five seconds or I'm going to throw you down on it."

Gabe reached for his pants and unfastened them, but before he removed them, he paused. Then he looked at me with a half-smile. "Throw me down on it you say?"

"Gabe," I said, and my voice sounded strained even to my own ears.

"What? You brought it up."

With his pants now undone and hanging around his hips, he put a knee on the mattress and climbed onto it. I shoved a hand inside my pants and wrapped my fingers around my cock, giving it a firm stroke before freeing it from its tight confines.

"Okay, Mr. St. James. I'm here. Now what?"

Fucking hell, things were about to get out of control—fast.

CHAPTER 28
GABE

MARCUS ST. JAMES in a full tuxedo was one of the sexiest things I'd ever seen in my life. But Marcus St. James with his shirt hanging off his broad shoulders, showing a teasing strip of skin from his throat down to his blond treasure trail, was hands-down *the* sexiest thing I'd ever seen in my life.

With his thick cock jutting out of his pants as if it could no longer be contained, it was all I could do not to come from the sight. But I knew what he planned to do with that and how well he would do it, and I didn't care what I had to think about in order to keep myself in check. I would not miss out on having him inside me again.

"Come closer," Marcus said in a voice made for sin. "Take off my shirt,"

I slipped my hands under the material and sucked in a shaky breath. His skin was hot—there wasn't one thing about him that was cold—and as I smoothed my hands over his shoulders and his white shirt fell to the floor, I let out a groan. There was some ink swirling along the side of his right forearm, and finding that hiding under his shirt made him even fucking hotter.

The way we were positioned we were eye to eye, and Marcus's were as dark as I'd ever seen them before. I licked my lips and reached down to wrap a hand over his. The second my fingers touched his, though, he grabbed hold of my wrist and took my lips in a fierce kiss.

Needing to be closer, I moved to the edge of the bed, and a tortured growl filled the air as Marcus's naked cock rubbed against the hard-on trapped inside my pants.

Marcus tore his lips free and looked down at the wrist he was still holding. "You touch me like that right now and I'm going to come. I'd much rather do that inside you tonight."

He didn't have to tell me twice. I wanted the exact same thing. When he let go of my arm to reach for the necklace at my throat, I looked down to see him running his thumb over the pendant.

"This has something to do with your music, doesn't it?"

My breathing was coming faster now, my chest rising and falling, as I kneeled in front of him and nodded.

"Yes. It's a treble bass clef heart." I pointed to the longer, sleeker musical note. "This is the treble."

"And the other is the bass clef?"

"Yes."

"And this..." He let go of my necklace and trailed his

fingers down the center of my chest and over my ribs and outlined the tattoo there, making me shiver.

My heart thumped in time to my now-throbbing cock as he studied the composition and said, "This is beautiful."

"Thank you."

"We're going to talk, you and I." He brought his attention back to me and laid his hand over my heart. "After."

I swallowed at the genuine interest behind the arousal in his eyes and nodded. "After."

"But right now, get on your feet, Gabe."

The instruction was simple and the result sexy as hell. Marcus was a tall man, and when I shifted from my knees to my feet on the mattress, it put everything from my navel down at easy access—including my excited dick.

Marcus slipped his fingers into the elastic of my briefs then tugged them and my pants down to my ankles, where I raised each foot one at a time, eager to get rid of it all. Tonight it felt different; tonight I felt like he was seeing more of me than he ever had before.

"Gorgeous," he said, more to himself than me, as he smoothed his large hands around to my ass and drew me closer. I speared my fingers through his thick hair for something to hang on to, and when he leaned in and placed his lips against the musical notes decorating my torso, my hips automatically thrust forward.

His tongue flicked out, and then he drew it up to one of my nipples and sucked it between his lips. I ground my hips against him, rubbing my leaking shaft all over his skin, and the thought of leaving my mark, my scent, on his body made me grind my hips a little harder.

A throaty groan filled the air as Marcus scraped his teeth across my nipple, and when I tightened my fingers in his hair, he switched to the other side. The hands on my ass flexed and spread my cheeks apart as his fingers began to flirt with the shadowy cleft in between.

I could feel the sticky mess I was making all over him, but Marcus didn't seem to care. I continued to use him to get myself good and ready for whatever he had planned next. I shut my eyes and reveled in the feelings washing over me. When one of his fingers finally grazed my hole, a loud curse left my lips.

Marcus raised his head, and I opened my eyes to protest, but his fingers dug into my ass cheeks and he lifted me clear off the bed. The next thing I knew, I was flat on my back, and he was climbing over me like a lion stalking its prey.

With his golden hair messed up from my hands and high color on his cheeks, Marcus was all sex and power in that moment, and I wanted to be taken over by him.

I parted my legs and watched with eager anticipation as he made his way up my body. The muscles in his arms bunched and flexed as he held himself above me and teased his tongue up my inner thigh. When he reached my cock and treated it to the same wicked torment, a shout flew off my tongue and echoed around his room.

Marcus continued his way up my body, and when he finally planted his hands by my head, I reached down and slid my hands in under his loose pants. I dug my fingers into his ass and rolled my hips up, and when I finally rubbed my sticky shaft along his, Marcus groaned and kissed me by my ear.

"You look fucking good in my bed. Better than I ever imagined."

I turned my head to look him in the eye. "And how many times did you imagine it?"

"Every goddamn night since we met."

Fuck that was hot. To think that someone as incredible as Marcus couldn't get me off his mind was a huge stroke to my...ego, and I couldn't help but grin.

"You like that?" he said, and trailed his fingers down my cheek to my mouth. "You like that I've lain here every night and thought about how it was going to feel to slide back inside you again?"

"Hell yes."

Marcus pressed his index finger to my lower lip. "Good, because I'm about to find out."

I was panting now as I stared up at him, ready and willing for whatever was going to happen next. But when he pulled back and climbed off the bed, I almost cried out.

I shifted to my elbows, not willing to take my eyes off him for even a second. Marcus kicked out of his shoes, shoved out of his pants, and finally stood before me as naked as I was.

Holy shit. Marcus in clothes was one sexy fucking man. Marcus *without* clothes was enough to make my brain explode. From his long legs, to his thick, erect cock, to his muscular torso and broad shoulders, Marcus was a prime example of the male form. One I wanted to study in detail, up close and personal.

I reached for my dick and wrapped a tight fist around it, worried I was about to come from just the sight of him. But when Marcus walked over to a dresser and pulled out a bottle of lube and condom, any idea of finishing this without him vanished.

Without a word, he was back on the bed and kneeling between my thighs, and when he tore the packet open and rolled the condom on, I trembled at what was about to happen next.

"Bend your legs," Marcus said, and flicked open the lid of the lube. "Put your feet flat on the bed, Gabe."

Oh fuck, *fuck*, I knew what was coming. At least I was pretty damn sure I did. The idea that Marcus was about to put his slippery fingers all over and inside me made flames lick all over my aroused body.

As I placed my feet flat on the mattress, the expression on Marcus's face was one of unadulterated lust. He looked like he wanted to devour me, and if he decided that was the better option this second, I wasn't going to stop him.

He licked his lips, and I pumped my hips up in response, the word "Please" falling from my tongue.

"Please what?" Marcus said as he poured some of the lube into the palm of his hand and tossed the bottle aside.

"Touch me."

Marcus drew his fingertip up the underside of my shaft. "Just *touch* you?"

My legs shook, and I widened them further for him, not

caring in the least how desperate it made me look. I wanted him, I'd never hidden that, and I'd do whatever it took now to get some part of him inside me.

"Stretch me," I said, looking him right in the eye. Then I remembered something he'd said that night in the studio. "Get me ready so you can take me *all* night. You wanted longer that first time round? Get me ready so I can give it to you."

"Fuck, Gabe." Marcus's jaw ticked as he looked over my naked body, then he stroked his slippery fingers along my shaft and wrapped his fist around me.

"That boldness, that confidence of yours"—he gave me a long, hard stroke—"don't ever lose it."

Not a chance, and now that I knew he liked it, I'd hold nothing back.

"Now back to that request of yours." Marcus smirked, and a delicious thrill of anticipation raced up my spine. "Pull your knees back for me. Let's get you ready."

CHAPTER 29

MARCUS

THIS HAD BEEN a long time coming. At least, that was how it felt as I stared down at the man splayed out naked on my bed.

With his knees spread and pulled back against his chest, Gabe was about as vulnerable as a person could be as I knelt between his thighs. Yet as he looked up at me from under those gorgeous lashes, all I saw was red-hot desire.

He was stunning, the very picture of sex and sensuality, and when I trailed my finger down the sensitive strip of skin leading to his tight entrance, he pressed his head back into the pillow and slammed his eyes shut.

His thick lashes gently kissed the skin just above his cheekbones, and the sheer beauty of him took my breath away. It had been that way from the very beginning with Gabe. One look at him and I'd been entranced, one taste and I'd been hooked, and no matter how I'd tried to fight, deny, and ignore him, the truth of the matter was that I wanted him. Not just his body, but his company, and tonight it was time to enjoy both of those things.

I took hold of one of his ankles, knowing it was the best way to get his attention back on me, and when his eyes flicked open, I pressed the pad of one of my fingers to his tight little entrance. As I massaged the puckered skin, I turned my head and kissed him on the inside of his calf. He sucked in a breath and punched his hips up toward me, and as I kissed and licked my way up his leg, I pushed my finger past the first ring of muscle until it slipped inside.

"*Ahh*, Marcus," he said as I draped his leg over my shoulder. Then I slowly bent down until it was pushed back against his body.

I braced my palm on the mattress by his hip and pulled my finger free, then added a second until he arched off the bed and his body sucked both back inside. My dick became jealous as hell as I lowered my head and flicked my tongue over the tip of his cock, then I twisted and spread my fingers wide, stretching him nice and good.

"Fuck, you're so hot and tight, and…eager."

Gabe tightened the muscle my fingers were busy working on and nodded.

"So fucking eager."

"Jesus." At the end of my of control, I pulled my fingers free, and when Gabe's leg slipped off my shoulder, I was up and over him before he could blink. My lips met his, our tongues dueled, and when he wrapped his legs around my waist, I reached between us and positioned myself against that greedy body.

The second he felt me nudging against his hole, he tore his lips free and bit back a curse, then I braced my hands by his head and ever so slowly breached that first ring of muscle.

Gabe stared up at me, his expression blissed out, as all thought other than the pleasure his body was experiencing left and the dizzying rush of arousal took over.

"Marcus, God... Oh my fucking *God.*" He squeezed his eyes shut as he did his best to accommodate all of me. But when I reached for his hands and pressed them into the mattress by his head, his eyes quickly reopened.

"You can take me. I know you can," I said.

Gabe's chest rose under mine, and when he hooked his ankles over the curve of my ass and shoved his hips up, I slipped all the way inside, and the sexy flirt winked at me.

"That was never a question," he said as he rolled his hips, slipping a little way off me, before taking me back inside again. "I was just enjoying the *buuuurn.*"

How I'd ever thought I stood a chance of resisting him, I had no idea. But I was happy to be done with that ridiculous line of thinking. I entwined our fingers and began to finally move inside of him.

Gabe picked up on my rhythm as though we'd been doing this for years, and as we moved in time with one another, everything other than what we were feeling was now forgotten.

His heels were pressing into my ass, urging me in and out at the exact pace he wanted, and every time I hit just the right spot, Gabe's fingers tightened and his lips parted on a sexy gasp.

"Fuck you're good at that."

I kissed his mouth and sucked on his full lower lip. "I know."

Gabe grinned, and I couldn't remember ever having such a good time in bed. Hell, I couldn't remember having such a good time, period.

"Arrogant."

"Hmm," I said, and withdrew a little. "But right just the same." Then I thrust forward again, proving my point.

Gabe shouted, and his fingers damn near cut off the circulation from mine, at the same time his legs tightened around my waist. I could feel his excitement, warm and sticky, as it dripped from his cock onto my stomach, and I knew this wasn't going to last much longer.

I let go of one of his hands and took hold of his chin, and after a thorough kiss that left the both of us breathless, I reached down and wrapped a firm hand around him. As I began to stroke him in time with our bodies, Gabe's lips parted and he moaned in ecstasy. His warm breath against my skin made me move faster with every sound he made, and when I gave one final thrust and squeezed him tight, Gabe tensed.

He shouted out my name and came in a hot, hard rush, coating my fingers and our stomachs as his dick jerked in my hand. He trembled under me, pleasure racking his body over and over, and his legs slipped down from my waist and fell apart on the mattress.

He opened his eyes. "I can't feel my legs."

"Good, because you're not going anywhere yet."

His lazy, satisfied smile made me pull out of him and discard the condom quicker than I'd thought possible. Then, with a hand slick from his cum, I began to get myself off to the vision of him lying there, naked and spent in my bed.

Clearly understanding what I was doing, what was fueling my final high, Gabe placed his feet flat just like he had at the start of all of this, but this time the view was much different.

His body looked well used, well stretched, and well and truly fucked, and knowing that I had done that, coupled with the wicked expression on his gorgeous face, made my climax hit—and hit hard. My balls tightened, my body shook, and the next thing I knew, I was coming all over the gorgeous man smiling up at me like he'd just won the lottery.

As I floated down from the best high I'd ever had, Gabe relaxed into my bed like he owned the damn thing, and right now he just might—he'd certainly claimed a part of me.

"That was hot as hell. *We* are hot as hell." He let out a triumphant laugh and let his eyes rove down over me. "I told you."

My lips twitched despite myself, but before I could say a word, he shifted to his knees in front of me and whispered across my lips, "Tell me I'm wrong."

I gripped the back of his neck and pressed a hard kiss to his mouth. "I can't. I don't lie."

"Uh huh." Gabe grinned. "Hot. As. Hell."

He reached down to gently stroke my sensitive cock. I

ran my fingers through his hair, took a good hold of it, and then tilted his head back so he was looking at me.

"Gabe?"

"Hmm...?"

"I meant what I said just now. I don't lie." His eyes narrowed a fraction, and I chuckled. "I told you I wanted you *all* night."

I shoved him back on the bed, and when he laughed some more and rolled over, moving to his hands and knees, I couldn't help but swat him on the ass.

"Hot as hell is right," I finally agreed. "Now let's see if *you* were telling the truth. Can you give me all night?"

Gabe, being Gabe, glanced over his shoulder, winked, and said, "And twice in the morning if you ask me really nice."

Turned out he *was* telling truth, and I could—on occasion—be really, *really* nice.

CHAPTER 30

GABE

I N THE EARLY hours of Sunday morning, I woke to the soft sound of a cell phone vibrating on the nightstand. I yawned and rolled to my back, my well-used muscles reminding me of all the delicious ways Marcus had taken me the night before—aaand a couple of times this morning.

A smile crept onto my lips as the mattress dipped beside me, and a warm, naked body moved in against the side of mine as Marcus reached across me for the phone.

I opened my eyes to see his broad chest only inches from my face, and couldn't resist pressing my lips against all of that warm skin. The second he felt me, he paused with his hand on the phone and looked at me. My stomach flipped and I knew I was in so much trouble.

"Sorry," he said in that deep, gravelly voice that sent flames licking along my skin. "I forgot to move it to my side before we fell asleep."

"I'm not complaining. I woke up with you on top of me again. It's like I'm living a fantasy that never seems to end."

Marcus chuckled and moved back to his side of the bed, propping a couple pillows behind him so he could read whatever had just come through on his phone, and now that I was awake, there was no way I was letting him get too far away.

I scooted in close beside him, nestled in under his arm, and wondered, not for the first time in the past few hours, if this would be the moment that he would send me away—because it really did feel like a fantasy.

Not only had I been on the best date of my life last night, I'd come home and spent the rest of it in the arms—and bed—of my dream man. Marcus was smart, sophisticated, and every sexual fantasy I could ever want, and that all seemed a little too good to be true. So, yeah, call me crazy, but I was waiting for the other shoe to drop.

"A fantasy, huh?" Marcus placed the phone down on his nightstand and flicked on the lamp, and as it bathed the room in a soft, golden glow, he wrapped an arm around my shoulders and tugged me in close. "Then I must be right there in it with you."

My heart thumped impossibly faster as I tilted my head back to see if he was messing with me. But the expression on his face was dead serious, and that took my breath away. *I was Marcus St. James's fantasy. Now what would it take to become his reality?*

Not wanting to miss a second of this, I moved up and over him until Marcus parted his legs, and when I settled in between them and rested my cheek against his chest, the loud beat of his heart matched mine.

Gentle fingers stroked my hair and down to my neck, where Marcus squeezed and massaged the tense muscles before running his fingers back up to the longer strands on top. It was relaxing, soothing, and made me want to close my eyes and never leave.

"Did you fall back asleep?"

I turned my head and flicked my tongue over his nipple, and Marcus's fingers tightened in my hair.

"Well, that answers that question."

I grinned at him and Marcus cradled my face in his hands. He swept one of his thumbs over the top of my cheek and then down to my lips.

"What kind of spell have you weaved over me, Gabriel Romero?"

"No spell."

"No?"

"No." I closed my eyes and kissed his palm. "I'm just being myself."

"Well, yourself is pretty damn impressive."

The respect in his voice made me look back to him, but before I could respond, Marcus rolled us over until I was flat on my back and he was again hovering over the top of me.

My breathing was coming faster now as he stared down at me with an expression I couldn't quite decipher. Then he brushed my hair back from my face and grazed his lips across mine.

"You caught me completely off guard last night," he said. "I can't remember the last time that happened."

Feeling rather pleased with myself, I wound my arms around his neck and craned up to kiss him. "With my musical skill or—"

"*With* your musical skill." Marcus studied me closely, and I wondered for a second what it was he was looking for. "Why didn't you tell me you could play an instrument?"

That was easy enough. "You never asked."

"No, I don't suppose I did." My breath caught as he lightly brushed his thumb across my lips. "What other secrets are you keeping?"

I blinked and ran my hands through his hair. "No secrets. If you want to know something, ask and I'll tell you."

"Just like that?"

I nodded. "Just like that."

Marcus had such a great poker face that there was no guessing what he was thinking right then, but he knew how I felt and what I wanted. I'd been transparent from the very moment we'd met. Yes, I'd told a few white lies to get his attention, but I'd never denied how much I wanted him.

He, on the other hand, had been insistent that this weekend was just an extension of the deal we had struck. That the attraction between us could never amount to anything because I was too young and we had nothing in common. Last night that theory had been blown out of the water, and with every passing minute it became increasingly obvious that we more than enjoyed each other's company—

we were reveling in it. The only question now was, would Marcus ever admit it?

"Will you tell me about it?" His request was quiet, as though he wasn't sure he had a right to ask but was too curious not to. "How you learned to play like that? Why you aren't playing anymore?"

I shifted to my side, and when Marcus did the same, I took a second just to look at him, to marvel over the fact that I was in this man's bed, that he'd invited me here, and instead of kicking me out after he'd gotten what he wanted, he was asking me questions to get to know me better.

"Gabe?"

"Sorry, I'm still kind of stuck in that fantasy loop."

Marcus's lips curved. He was so damn handsome.

"Should I go and put on some clothes? Will that help you focus?" As he went to throw the covers back and sit up, I grabbed his arm and tugged him back down.

"Don't you dare. I was just admiring the view, but let's see. Me and music, where to start..." I thought back to the first Christmas concert my yaya took me to and smiled. "It would have to be the *Nutcracker* at Chicago's Auditorium Theatre."

"The ballet?"

"Yeah, but I was more intrigued by the people sitting under the stage in the orchestra pit. I thought it was so cool. Everything went dark, but they had these little lights showing them what to play and where their instruments were at. It was like a secret fort or something. I was fascinated. But I was also, like...eight."

Marcus smiled, and the expression in his eyes softened, making my chest tighten. "So was it always the cello?"

"Oh, God no." I laughed. "I'm sure my parents wished it was, but no. They had to go through years of me experimenting with one instrument to the next. I started with percussion, the cymbals and bongos. You can imagine my parents' delight when I decided that banging things together very loudly wasn't for me."

"Uh, that I can."

"Although it did help me get out a lot of my teenage angst."

"You were angsty?"

I held up my fingers an inch or two apart. "Maybe a little."

"I can't imagine that." Marcus took my hand in his and drew my finger to his lips. "You seem so happy, so full of life."

"So...energetic?"

"Mhmm, that too. So, what came after the percussion?"

I screwed my nose up. "The brass section."

"Really?"

"Yeah... Specifically, the trumpet, until, um, one day I came home and my mom all but begged me to stop. I can still hear her now: '*Cualquier otra cosa, Gabriel. Cualquier cosa menos eso.*' Which translates to: 'Anything else, Gabriel. Anything but that.'"

Marcus laughed, a full, deep, robust laugh that I couldn't help but reciprocate. "She sounds like a smart lady."

"She is, very smart. Because of her, I started to experiment with the strings family, and then one day I found the cello."

"And how old were you then?"

"Um, sixteen?"

"Wow." Marcus nodded. "So just last year."

For a second the joke caught me off guard, his face was so serious, but when a teasing light entered his eyes, I shoved him in the arm. "Hilarious."

He chuckled. "So what about reading the music? Did that come easy for you?"

"For the most part, yeah. Don't ask me how or why; it just did. After that, my love affair with the cello began."

"Love affair, huh?"

"Oh yeah. We've had our up and downs for sure. She hurts me, I get mad—"

"She?"

"Don't get jealous."

"I'll try to contain myself."

"But yeah, she's snapped at me in public a few times."

Marcus's eyes widened, and I grinned.

"Her C-string, right there on stage. Once it even cut my cheek."

"Really?" He reached out to brush his thumb along my cheekbone. "I didn't realize playing the cello was so hazardous to your health."

"It can be for sure, and painful when you're starting out until you develop callouses. See?" I held my hand up, and Marcus inspected the hardened lines across my skin. They'd faded a little, since I wasn't playing as often, but they were still there.

"I feel like I've learned so much in the past few minutes. I didn't know any of that."

"Most don't. Occasionally, if you're sitting close enough, you'll see a violin, cello, or double bass string snap. But we're taught to keep going; you can't stop mid-performance. The show must go on."

"Unless you're missing an eye."

"Well, yeah, but thankfully, that never happened. Just a couple of cuts here and there."

The room fell quiet for a minute, and then Marcus said, "You played with the Chicago Symphony. Would I have seen you?"

I'd wondered that too, and depending on how often he attended the shows, it was definitely possible. I'd substituted a couple of times when one of the current members was unavailable, waiting for the day I graduated so I could take my permanent seat on that stage. But unfortunately, that day had never come.

"Maybe? I played a couple of times last year. If you went to all of the season ticket holder shows—"

"I did."

"Then you would've seen me."

"That seems impossible. That I would've seen you and —" Marcus cut himself off, and then asked, "Why don't you play anymore?"

I'd known that question was coming. But the idea of having to say it out loud brought my new reality back to the forefront, when tonight I'd been riding high in my fantasy world.

When I didn't immediately answer, Marcus squeezed my hand. "I'm sorry. You don't have to tell me. It's none of my business. I was just curious because you're so talented. It seems like such a shame that you weren't up there on that stage."

"It is a shame." I tipped my face back so I could look him in the eye. "But if I'd been up there, I wouldn't have been with you, and I wouldn't have traded tonight for anything."

"Not even a cello seat in Chicago's Symphony?" Marcus arched a brow. "That wouldn't be a smart move."

"Okay, well, let's not get crazy. But life has a different path for me now. I've come to accept that. After the accident, I had to."

"You mentioned that earlier. The accident. Can I ask what happened?"

"Yeah, of course. It was stupid. I had a week off over fall break and decided to go on a motorcycle trip with a friend. We were going to take a ride from Chicago to Starved Rock National Park. There's some beautiful scenery on that route, and this small town where we could stop and refuel before coming home. Long story short, I wasn't all that experienced and got a little overconfident."

"*You*, overconfident? Never."

I let out a sigh and shook my head. "Yeah, well, I shouldn't have been in this case. The engine was more powerful than I really knew how to handle, and when it took off, I fell and put my left hand out to catch myself. I fractured several bones in my hand, including the scaphoid bone at the base of my thumb, and had to have a full cast fitted to my wrist for the following eight weeks. I lost my scholarship, my physical conditioning, and any hopes of graduating all from one stupid mistake, and in the end, I had to drop out of my course a year early."

Marcus frowned, and the pity in his eyes was almost too much to bear. "There was no way to let you onto the symphony anyway? I hardly think a piece of paper confirms whether or not you're an accomplished player."

"It doesn't, but it helps. Plus, I'd lost all of the conditioning I would need to play professionally. One day I'll audition for them again. But I'm not ready yet. I'm not sure when I will be. Having to take such an extensive sabbatical caused my muscles to get weak, for my skill level to drop, and until that's up to par again, I have no business being on that stage. Tonight was just a one-off."

"Tonight was brilliant." Marcus tilted my face up to his, and the seriousness in his gaze only underlined the conviction in his voice. "*You* are brilliant, and I know that one day you'll get back there."

"So do I. I'll also finish my degree, but not today." When Marcus merely looked at me, I grinned. "I have to save up for tuition first."

"Hence the new job."

"Hence the new job."

Marcus traced his fingers along my jaw and then outlined my lips. "Thank you for telling me."

"Like I said, you ask, I'll answer. No secrets here."

He nodded then shifted in the bed until we were again lying on our sides facing one another. "I know I said I'd let you go home Monday, but I don't want you to go."

I scooted in close to him until I could slip a leg between his and kiss his chin. "No?"

"No." Marcus wrapped his arms around me and brushed his lips over the top of my hair. "I want to keep you."

I trembled in his arms and wondered how I was supposed to think when he was saying things like that.

"Gabe?"

"Hmm?"

"Say you'll stay with me."

I tipped my face up to look into his eyes, and the emotions swirling there made the breath catch in the back of my throat. Something was happening here, something big, and there was no way I was leaving without finding out what it was.

"For how long?"

Marcus's eyes blazed when he realized I wasn't saying no.

"Until Thursday," he whispered. "That's the end of your week, and the end of our deal."

I was about to ask him, *And then what?* But before I could, Marcus took my lips in a kiss that claimed me, and my only thought after that was: *How do I make him want to keep me forever?*

CHAPTER 31

MARCUS

"WHAT TIME DO you need to be at work this morning?"

Gabe looked up at me with water droplets clinging to his lashes as the warm shower spray hit the middle his back.

"Hmm." He sidled in close, his hands on my chest drawing circles in the soapy suds waiting to be rinsed off. "By eight thirty, but I like to get there a little earlier so I'm there before Logan."

I brought the sponge up to his shoulders and ran it down his chest to his abs, getting him nice and soaped up like he'd just done to me.

After Gabe had agreed to stay the full week, we'd spent all of Sunday in amongst the sheets getting to know one another from head to toe. It was—if my memory served me correct—the first Sunday in years that I had not opened my computer, my emails, or turned on the news. I'd decided to live inside that little fantasy world with Gabe for a day longer, and only respond if an SOS came through on my phone.

Fortunately for me, the world had continued to turn without my assistance. But now that Monday was here, there was no escaping the jobs we both had to go back to, and for the first time ever, I found myself resentful of the interruption.

"And do you like it?" I asked, moving the sponge around to his back and working it over the smooth skin. "Working for Logan?"

"Yeah, he's great. I think he's still feeling me out a little, though."

My hand paused on Gabe's ass. "Feeling you out?"

Gabe licked his wet lips, and my dick took great interest as he slid his hands over my shoulders and fingered the back of my hair.

"As in my *personality*. Relax, Mr. St. James. Logan is very married and very much in the boss box."

"The boss box?"

"Yeah, as in, do not touch. Do not pass go. Do not think of anything down below."

I scoffed and slowly stroked the sponge up his back again. "I think that's a great motto."

"Oh yeah? I mean, technically, you should be in that box too, *buuut* I decided to make an exception for you."

"Did you now?"

"Mhmm." Gabe nipped at my chin and then kissed his way up to my ear. "You know, since you're not really my boss, more like my...master."

I tossed the sponge to the tiled floor and walked him back under the spray to the wall. "Master, huh?"

His eyes darkened as he ran them down over me, and when they landed on my now-stiff cock, he grinned. "You ask, I shall obey."

Gabe was about as submissive as I was, but the twinkle in his eyes told me he was in the mood to play. My eyes roamed down his slick, wet skin, and I figured if we were quick about it, we could get in an early-morning workout.

I rinsed off under the spray, running a hand through my hair so I could keep a close eye on him, and then I moved to the glass door and said, "Your turn. Rinse off and I'll be right back. And when I return, the only words I want to hear out of your mouth are 'yes, Mr. St. James.'"

Gabe shoved off the wall, stepped under the spray, and grinned as he stroked his eager erection. As I walked out of the shower to go and get what we needed, the cocky little shit called after me, "Yes, Mr. St. James." And I couldn't help but think that this was how I should *always* start off my workweek.

I STEPPED OFF the elevator with a little more enthusiasm than a usual Monday morning inspired and headed over to Carmen, who was on the phone behind her desk.

"Good morning, Carmen," I said with a smile.

With a confused look on her face, Carmen ceased

talking on the phone. I glanced at the leather binder that housed the hard copy of my schedule and pointed to it.

"Can I have that for a second, please?"

"Um, sure." She blinked a couple of times, then, without saying goodbye, hung up. "Is, uh, everything okay, sir?"

"Everything is fine," I said as she handed over the schedule. "What about you? Is everything okay here? Did you have a good weekend?"

Shock flashed across Carmen's face, but as I reached for the pen in my jacket, she'd schooled her features to neutral.

"It was fine. How—" She cleared her throat. "How was yours?"

"I had a very...*fun* weekend," I said, and smiled again, thinking of this morning in the shower.

"I'm glad to hear it. Is there something I can help you with on the schedule? Something you need moved?"

I skimmed over the next few days and nodded. "Yes, actually. I'd like to rearrange a few things if I could. I want to be out of here no later than four thirty this week."

"Four thirty?"

"Yes, and on Wednesday, let's make it four."

"Oh, okay." Carmen nodded. "I'll reschedule anything that needs moving and run it by you as soon as I have the new times."

"Fantastic." I tapped her desk and was about to walk off when I remembered something. "Oh, and I'm expecting a call from Giles Vanderhall this morning from New York. If you could put him through immediately, that would be appreciated."

"Of course, sir."

"Very good—okay then. Well, if you need me—"

Carmen narrowed her eyes, and I realized that in all the time she'd been employed here, I'd never once asked her that. Figuring I might've just offended her, I decided the best thing I could do was leave.

"Okay, I'll be in my office."

She nodded, and as I headed down the hall, I could feel her eyes on me. This was why I never engaged in small talk. I should've just called her up and asked her to make the change, but my good mood had made me more amiable than usual, and I'd decided to step out of my comfort zone for a minute. Look where that got me.

I'd just finished booting up my computer when my phone began to vibrate on my desk. When I saw Gabe's name flashing across the screen, I smiled, hit *accept*, then turned in my chair to look out at the lake below.

"Aren't you supposed to be at work, young man?"

"Funny thing about that. Some bossy know-it-all assured me that it wouldn't take more than ten minutes to get across town when he left me in the back of his Escalade this morning. It's been fifteen minutes now and I'm stuck behind a traffic accident. Want to guess where I still am?"

I glanced at the clock to see it was just turning eight twenty-five. Gabe was right—he was running late.

"Only one block from the ENN building," he said.

I grimaced. "Are you going to get in trouble?"

"Honestly? I have no idea. If Logan didn't fire me for, um, well, you know—"

"Impersonating him?"

"*Yes*ss. I'm not sure how he'll react to me being late."

Shit. I hated that I'd put him in that situation, even though I'd thoroughly enjoyed the reason why, and just as I was about to apologize, Gabe asked, "What would you do?"

"If I was running late?"

Gabe sighed. "No. What would you do if you were Logan and I was running late?"

"Oh, that's easy, I'd fire you." The line went silent, and when several seconds passed and Gabe said nothing, I started to laugh.

"I hate you."

"No you don't."

"Yes, I really think I hate you right this second."

He sounded so irritated and put out that I couldn't help but tease him a little more. "Well, how about you get to work, apologize profusely, and if you get fired, text me and I'll have Franklin come pick you up."

"If I get *fired*, it'll be your fault. You know that, right?"

"Actually, I think it'd be your fault, because you looked so fucking sexy this morning that I couldn't let you leave without giving you a proper send-off."

Gabe groaned, and I imagined him shutting his eyes and licking those luscious lips. "I have to go. I need to get decent for when we get through this damn traffic. The last thing I need is to walk in late, hard as a rock."

"Gabe?"

"Hmm?"

"He won't fire you. If he's smart, he'll make you grovel a

little, and that way you'll never want to do it again. That's what I'd do."

"Thanks for that."

"Oh, one last thing. Do you cook?"

"Uh, I can grill a mean steak."

"Good, then that's what's for dinner."

"Dinner?"

"Yes, you're cooking. Don't forget, you still have four days left under my thumb."

Gabe scoffed. "Last time I checked, it wasn't your thumb I was under."

That was true. But a deal was a deal, and I wanted to make sure that neither of us forgot that. I could already see how easy it would be to slip into something more with Gabe. But the reality was that anything *more* was not in the cards for someone like me.

"Send me a list of what you need, and have a good day at work. I'll see you at five."

"Five? But you always work late."

"Not this week I'm not. I'll see you at five, Gabe."

"I'll see you then, Mr. St. James."

I swear I could hear a smile in his voice as he said that, and just as I ended the call, my office phone began to ring. I moved back to my desk and picked up the receiver.

Carmen said in my ear, "Mr. Vanderhall is on the line."

"Thank you, Carmen. You can put him through."

"Yes, sir."

I pulled up the email I'd received last week from the CEO of Summit Broadcasting, and when the line connected, I sat back and greeted my longtime acquaintance.

"Giles, how are you doing over there in the Big Apple this morning?"

"Good, Marcus, good, and you? How's Chicago treating you?"

"I can't complain."

"No, you certainly can't." Giles laughed. "Congratulations on your ratings this quarter. Gloria must be beside herself."

"She's certainly not crying herself to sleep at night, that's for sure."

"I wouldn't be either. Top three news anchors and top two news shows—that's a tight ship you're running over there, and a winning one at that. Although that Brian Evans mess was...less than ideal."

It was always interesting to me how job interviews and contract negotiations went, as far as the broadcasting world at the top of the food chain. The company CEO would charm and schmooze you, but at the same time casually remind you that you weren't perfect and there were always other fish in the sea.

I'd been through this a couple of times before, however, and I was well aware of what I brought to the table. I was—what did Gabe call me?—a big fucking fish when it came to this world, and Giles knew he'd be lucky to catch me. That was why he'd been the first to throw out a line.

"There's always something coming up in this industry, Giles, you know that. Always some sort of fire to put out."

"That's true, and no one puts them out better than you. I haven't seen hide nor hair of Evans in days."

Damn right he hadn't. After that stunt Brian pulled, he'd been yanked from the air, all reports about him had been deflected to something bigger and more sensational, and this morning there was barely a whisper about him.

That was the way it worked in the news and entertainment business. If what you did wasn't illegal and you could hold out and take an extended vacation, the likelihood was high that someone with a bigger and more interesting issue than you would come along, and hey presto, they'd take your place on the shit list.

"I doubt you called wanting to speak about Brian Evans, Giles. So why don't you tell me what this is really about?"

"Don't play coy, Marcus. It doesn't suit you. You know everyone's looking at your resumé right now with your contract about to be up. And with the ratings at ENN being what they are, you've got the pick. I just want to make sure that Summit is on your radar."

Oh, it was on my radar, all right. New York, that was the pinnacle—the dream all reporters have when they start out. The problem was that I was no longer an up-and-coming reporter. I was the president of the news division in the number one news broadcasting company in the country, and it was going to take a hell of a lot to make me bite.

That didn't mean I wasn't hungry.

I sat back in my chair and drummed my fingers on the desk. "It is on my radar, but I want to know more before I make any decisions. Send me over what you're thinking, let me take a look at it, and I'll get back to you."

There was a pause, and then he said, "Okay. That's fair. I'll get something together and send it your way by the end of the day. But don't make me wait too long, Marcus. You might be on top right now. But as you know, if you stand still for too long in this business, the wind will change."

Nothing like a veiled threat to motivate a person. But if he thought that would somehow worry me, he was mistaken. I never made an impulsive or rushed decision when it came to my career, and I wasn't about to start now.

"Like I said, send it over and I'll take a look. I have to go. We'll talk soon."

"Count on it," he said, and then ended the call.

I clicked open my email and saw messages from at least three more of the big broadcasting companies sitting in my inbox, each requesting a call sometime this week, and I forwarded the ones that I was interested in to Carmen to set up a date.

My contract with Tennant Broadcasting was up next month, and I really needed to start thinking about what I wanted next out of my life when it came to the news world. I'd built one hell of career and reputation for myself over the years, and now I was being offered an opportunity to grow it again.

The real question was: where was the best opportunity to do that, and how much were they willing to pay me to get me there?

CHAPTER 32
GABE

I WAS LATE. Not terribly late, but late just the same, and when the elevator doors to Mitchell & Madison slid open, I raced across the lobby toward the glass doors.

"Morning, Gabe," Tiffany called out as I flew by her and threw a quick wave in her direction, and then continued down the hall toward my desk.

This was Marcus's fault. I mean, really, it was probably mine, because I'd suggested that we should conserve water by showering together. But if he'd been quick about getting inside me, instead of taking his sweet, delicious time about it, then I wouldn't be racing down the hall this morning like my ass was on fire.

Sure, I'd have a permanent smile on my face for the rest of the day, but the entire elevator ride up here I'd been praying that Logan had somehow gotten held up in the same traffic jam as I had on his way into work this morning.

When I reached my desk and glanced inside his office,

however, I realized I was out of luck. He was already inside, but he wasn't alone like I'd expected him to be. Instead, a man with a head full of dark curls sat in one of the chairs opposite his desk as Logan unpacked his briefcase.

I quickly dumped my bag on the ground and pulled up Logan's schedule, then let out a quick sigh of relief when I saw that it was empty until ten. *Thank God.* At least I hadn't missed greeting a client.

I was just about to fall down into my chair when line one on my phone lit up, and I looked through the glass to see Logan was still talking to the man but now had the receiver to his ear.

Shit. This wasn't going to be good.

I snatched up the phone, and before I could say good morning, I heard, "You're late."

I grimaced and looked back through the glass, fully expecting Logan to be glaring me down. But his attention was still one hundred percent on the man opposite him.

"I'm sorry. It won't happen again." I grabbed up a pad of paper and pen. "What can I get for you?"

"*You* in here, pronto. That would be most helpful."

"Of course. Sorry. I'll be right there." As I hung up the phone and got to my feet, I cursed myself out. Then I headed to Logan's door—knocked, just to be polite—and entered when he gestured that I should.

As I walked inside, the man with all the curls finally turned around, and my feet faltered a little before coming to a dead stop. The guy was, well, really good-looking, in a leather-jacket-and-jeans kind of way.

"Ahh," Logan said, recapturing my attention. "It's so nice of you to join us today, Gabe."

I blinked and was about to apologize for the second time when the guy with the curls chuckled and got to his feet.

"Give him break, Logan. He's only five minutes late. And the last time I checked, you hadn't started work yet either."

"Only because *someone* was lingering in my office to avoid a meeting with the tax accountant."

The man glanced over his shoulder at my boss. "Are you complaining?"

Logan smirked. "Never."

"That's what I thought," the stranger said, before he turned his attention back to me and held out his hand. "Hi, I'm Tate, your boss's husband. You must be Gabe. My… pretend husband."

Oh shit. Okay, so not a client. But I wasn't sure this was better. I reached out and shook Tate's hand.

"Yeah, about that… I'm sorry." I aimed a tentative smile at Logan. "And I'm also sorry I'm late."

Jesus, just shoot me now.

Logan arched a brow. "Was it for a good reason?"

I thought about Marcus's slippery hand around my cock and his wet lips against mine, and before I could answer, a chuckle filled the room.

"You got laid this weekend."

"Logan," Tate said, his head snapping around to his husband.

"What? I've been on my best behavior for two weeks

now around him. It's exhausting. If Gabe's going to work for me then he needs to know what he's getting into."

"Oh God. Here we go," Tate muttered, as Logan came around his desk.

"Look," Logan said. "I think it's about time that you met the real me, and basically—"

"The real him has no filter," Tate said.

"I was going to put it more delicately than that."

"Then you would've been lying," Tate said, and I had to bite back a laugh. It was clear this discussion was one that came up often.

"*Any*way." Logan looked to me. "Everyone at this law firm knows I have a mouth on me, and it's been absolutely killing me to have to pretend that I don't. Sherry worked with me for years and knew me well. She knew the kind of..."

As Logan thought over his next words, Tate chimed in again. "The kind of pain-in-the-ass, completely inappropriate boss he could be. What he's basically trying to say is, he doesn't mean to offend you but probably will at least three times a day."

"Really, Tate, you're not helping—"

"Actually," I said, "that's kind of a relief."

The two of them looked at me, and I grinned.

"I've been trying to so hard to be professional every second I'm here, and you're right, it's exhausting. I'm never this—"

"Uptight? Studious? Quiet?" Logan said.

"Yes, exactly. I mean, I can be. But *I'm* usually the one without the filter."

"Ah ha! See," Logan said to Tate. "Not everyone is a prude. He doesn't care that I know he got laid."

"I really don't." I laughed. "But I am curious *how* you know."

"Oh God." Tate smiled and shook his head. "Don't encourage him."

But judging by Logan's smirk, it was too late. "See the relaxed, easygoing smile on Tate's face right now?"

"Yeah."

"When you walked in this morning, you looked just like him, and he got laid *several* times this weekend."

Tate rolled his eyes. "Yep, there you go."

Logan leaned over and kissed Tate's cheek. "I do so love making you smile."

Tate chuckled and looked at me. "You sure you want to work for this guy?"

When Logan grinned, all of the seriousness, all of the stand-up professionalism he'd showed since I'd started here, went out the window, and in its place was the mischief-making guy from Friday afternoon who'd told me to go and find the *Almighty* and shout out to God.

In fact, he reminded me a lot of myself.

"The last time I heard, I was his bitch, so I'm not going anywhere," I said.

"There you go." Logan shoved Tate in the arm, and then walked over to me. "We're going to get along just fine."

Tate looked between the two of us. "I don't know if I

should be happy or scared at the similarities I'm seeing here. But Gabe, if he ever drives you to drink, be sure to come down and see me at The Popped Cherry. I'll make sure to give *him* the tab."

Okay, Tate was super cool. Not only did he give Logan as good as he got, he was friendly and so easy to be around.

Figuring I'd taken up enough of their time together, I looked to my boss and said, "Would you like a coffee? Or anything else before you get started?"

Logan eyed me for a second, and I wondered if he would send me on some foolish quest as payment, but instead he shook his head.

"No, I'm fine. But if you could pull up the Bristol case and get ready to come in here and take notes, I'll just say goodbye to Tate and then we can get started."

"Sounds good." I looked at Tate and smiled. "It was nice to meet you."

"You too, and good luck with this one."

I thanked him again and hurried out to get myself organized. After I'd pulled the file and gotten everything I needed together, Logan's door pushed open and Tate walked out.

He came over and stopped at my desk, and when I glanced up at him, he gestured over his shoulder with his thumb.

"He's ready for you when you are. Oh, and Gabe? I really meant what I said—you should come down to The Popped Cherry one night. It's a great place to bring a date. There's drinking and dancing. What more could you want?"

A guy that actually wants *to date?* The second that popped into my head, I frowned, and Tate held up his hand.

"Hey, no pressure," he said, clearly misunderstanding. "It's just an offer."

"No, I— Sorry," I said, and let out a sigh. "It's just the guy I'm with, or interested in, he's a workaholic and isn't into the whole dating thing."

Okay, that sounded kind of weird and pathetic when I said it out loud. But instead of looking confused, or sorry for me, Tate chuckled and looked through the glass to where Logan stood with his cell phone to his ear.

"Don't let that line of talk stop you. I seem to remember a certain lawyer who didn't like to *date* either, and he's a happily married man now."

Logan? Really? But he seemed so happy, so settled.

Tate grinned and waved. "Have a good day, Gabe."

"Yeah, you too," I said as he walked off down the hall, and that glimmer of hope that a week wasn't *all* I'd get with Marcus flickered again in the back of my mind.

CHAPTER 33

MARCUS

THE SMELL OF sizzling-hot steak wafted into the kitchen as Gabe opened one of the double doors and made his way over to the counter.

He'd changed after work into a pair of khaki shorts and a long-sleeve red Henley, and the sound of his flip-flops against the tiled floor made me think of summertime and days at the beach, which was crazy, because I wasn't the kind who ever took vacations.

"Do you have one of those flippy things in here?"

As he mimicked the move with a flat hand, I opened a drawer to pull out the utensil he was referring to. "A spatula?"

"Yeah, that's it." He went to reach for it, and as he did, I tried reaching for him. But Gabe made a stealthy sidestep and pointed the spatula my way. "Hands off the cook, Mr. St. James. I'm carrying out an order and I will not be distracted."

"Is that right?"

"Yes, it is."

He winked at me and then turned to head back to the double doors, but before he disappeared outside, I called out, "Do you want anything to drink with your dinner?"

"Do you have wine?"

"Wine?" I didn't know why, but the request caught me completely off guard.

"Yes, you know. It's made from grapes."

"Yes smart-ass, I have wine. What kind do you like?"

"With a steak? *Red*. Come on, Marcus, even someone as young as me knows that."

I balled up the dishtowel and threw it at him, and after Gabe laughed and draped it over his shoulder to walk outside, I headed through to the wine cellar to give myself a moment.

Jesus, what the hell did I think I was doing? Playing house with a man half my age. It hadn't even occurred to me that he might like a glass of wine with dinner, and that was a wake-up call to our differences.

I needed to get a handle on myself. I needed to remember why Gabe was out on my deck cooking me dinner, and that only days from now he would be leaving. But that was easier said than done, and whenever he smiled and laughed like he had no problem he couldn't overcome, I found myself wishing I could hold on to that joy, hold on to *him* a little longer.

That was impossible, though. I knew who I was. I knew my track record when it came to relationships, and never had it included being the wonderful and attentive boyfriend. My relationships—if they could even be called that—never ended well, and nothing about this, *us*, led me to believe that I could keep him smiling the way he'd just been, and I wouldn't be the one to take that away from him.

One week. Thursday. That was the day we'd agreed upon. I'd do good to remember that, because the alternative had disaster written all over it.

I grabbed a bottle of wine and walked back into the kitchen to hunt down a couple of glasses. That was when Gabe stuck his head inside and grinned at me.

"It's ready."

I gestured to the bottle and glasses. "Can you grab those? I'll get the salad."

"Hmm, a Malbec. That's a good choice," he said as we headed back outside, where he pulled out a chair on one side of the table for me. "Welcome to Romero's Steakhouse."

I walked over, and before he moved away, I leaned in and snuck a soft kiss across his lips. He smiled, and returned it, before he took a step back, and I placed the salad down on the table.

I reached for the bottle of wine and uncorked it as he served up the steak, and just as I finished pouring his glass, Gabe placed a perfectly cooked New York strip in front of me. It looked and smelled delicious. When he took a seat on the opposite side of the table, my only complaint was that he was too damn far away.

He settled in and then passed the salad my way, and

after we'd each gotten what we wanted, he picked up his glass and swirled it before bringing it up under his nose.

I arched a brow, impressed. "You know your wines?"

Gabe grinned. "No. But I enjoy messing with you." He chuckled. "You should see your face right now. Relax, I'm not a secret wine connoisseur at the age of twenty-two."

"Oh God." I shook my head. "Every time you say that number—"

"You think what great shape you must be in that you wore *me* out yesterday?"

I laughed despite myself. "Not exactly where I was going with that."

"And yet it really should've been." Gabe took a sip and then nodded. "It's good. I like it. But honestly, a red is a red to me. I just know what color it is and if it's sweet or dry."

"Well"—I picked up the black pepper and ground some over my meal—"if you ever want to learn more, I have a whole cellar."

"Of course you do."

"Of course."

"You, me, and several bottles of wine?" Gabe cut into his steak. "Now that sounds like a lesson I'd like to take part in."

So would I. But it was hard to imagine he'd learn much in the next few days. "Okay, let's see how this steak is."

"See how it *is*? It's a perfect medium rare, as requested."

"I like your confidence, but can you back it up?"

Gabe gestured to my plate. "Try it and tell me I'm wrong."

If I'd learned anything about Gabriel Romero in the last

few days it was that whatever he did, he did well, and there was good reason for that. He was quick, smart, and remarkably self-assured for someone so young, and so far, he'd been able to back it up and then some.

I cut off a piece of the meat and popped it in my mouth, and sure enough, it was perfectly cooked. It was juicy, tender, and full of flavor.

"Well, how is it?"

I could've lied, but he never would've believed me. "It's a perfect medium rare."

"Told you."

"That you did. Is there anything you don't do well?"

Gabe shrugged. "Lie, apparently. But that got me here, so I'm going to go out on a limb and say I did that pretty well too."

Cocky. But I couldn't argue with him, because while I'd been infuriated by what he did that night, he was right—it had landed him here on my patio. I couldn't help but wonder if I would've walked away had I known the truth.

"You're thinking too hard," he said as I picked up my glass of wine and took another sip. "Are you still mad I lied to you that night?"

"Actually, I was just thinking the opposite."

"Oh yeah?"

"Yeah. I was thinking that had you approached me as yourself and I'd made assumptions based off your age, I probably would've walked away." Gabe took another bite of his meal and nodded, but said nothing. But I needed him to understand. "That would've been my loss."

Gabe swallowed and looked at me with a soft expression that I couldn't quite decipher, but it made my stomach twist and something inside my chest tighten. No other words were spoken as we finished our meal, but I was hit with the realization that I'd never been happier to be in someone's company than I was tonight.

When our plates were empty and so were our wineglasses, Gabe picked up the bottle and got to his feet. He made his way over to one of the couches lining the deck and then patted the spot beside him. "Bring the glasses?"

I did as he requested, and as I sank down into the seat beside him, Gabe poured the wine and then placed the empty bottle on the end table beside him.

"This deck is so beautiful at night." He rested his head back against a cushion and looked up at the sky. "All of these twinkle lights strung up and the planters all lit. It's like none of the buildings around you exist and the sky is right there within touching distance."

He reached up above himself as though trying to touch the stars.

"You're right, but I don't usually spend that much time out here at night," I said.

Gabe turned his head on the cushion to face at me. "Really?"

"Really. I'm usually in my office or the living room, working."

"I guess that makes sense, but why not work out here? It's like your own private oasis."

"I just never thought of it, I guess."

"Of course you didn't." Gabe chuckled and took a sip of his wine. "You're all work and no play, Mr. St. James. That's why you need someone like me in your life."

I knew he was being flippant, teasing me just for fun. But when Gabe looked at me again, and that same expression from earlier swirled in his eyes, I suddenly understood what I was seeing—hope—and I didn't have a clue what to do with that.

I sat up and reached for his glass to place it on the end table, and once his hands were free, I drew him to me until he was straddled over my lap and his arms were resting loosely around my neck.

While *hope* was too complicated an emotion to delve into, want and desire I could handle.

With his knees tucked in on either side of my hips, I cupped his ass and tugged him forward until his face was only inches from mine.

"You know, I would've said anything to get close to you that night, and look at me now," he said, staring down into my eyes. "The only thing I regretted was that you didn't know my real name."

"I know it now." I nipped at his lower lip and kissed my way along his jaw. "Gabe."

"Hmm," he said, his fingers teasing the hair at my nape. "Say it again."

I flicked my tongue across his earlobe and whispered, "Sexy, sweet Gabe."

He leaned back to look down at me and cradled my face in his hands. "Now that sounds good."

"Agreed. Dinner was wonderful, thank you."

"You're welcome anytime. Even *without* a deal to fulfill."

There it was again. That teasing note in his voice, that hopeful light shining in his eyes, and before I knew what I was doing, my mouth was making promises I knew I'd never be able to keep.

"About that." I ran a hand up his back to his neck. "What if we say it's already been fulfilled?"

"What has?"

"The deal."

Gabe froze and looked down at me. "But... Are you sure?"

"Yes. I like having you here."

"I like being here."

"Good. Then stay for the next few days just because of that. No strings, no deal, no pressure. Let's just enjoy each other."

Gabe's eyes lit up with pure happiness, and a niggling feeling of guilt washed over me. That was soon shoved aside, though, when he kissed me on the lips.

"Yes."

"Yes?"

"*Yesss*." He laughed, nodding enthusiastically.

"Okay. Then I have one other thing to ask, and feel free to say no, because it's *not* an order."

"Oh, this sounds mysterious."

"Trust me, it's not. My sister has a book launch on

Wednesday that she asked me attend. I was wondering if you'd like to go with me."

Gabe studied me for a minute and then asked, "As in...a date?"

Shit. Clearly I hadn't thought that through, but, quick as always, Gabe had seen an opportunity and run with it, and who was I to deny him that victory? For the next few days he'd agreed to be mine, and this was something I could give him that would make him happy. So in the end, I gave this round to him.

"Yes, as in a date."

CHAPTER 34

GABE

Turned out Marcus's sister only lived a couple of blocks over from me in one of the tallest buildings on the block. There were two of them, actually, side by side, guarding the neighborhood like towering soldiers, and each of them housed luxury condominiums, if you could afford it and that was your kind of thing.

Personally, the second I could get away from sharing a wall with someone else, I was doing it. I couldn't begin to count the number of times I'd had people bang on a wall or floor with a broomstick telling me to shut up while I tried to practice, and let's just say there's nothing like a little bit of ambient anger to really get you in the mood.

"Are you ready?" Marcus squeezed my hand, and the question along with the reassuring move made my heart thump a little harder.

I still couldn't quite believe that I was out on a date with Marcus St. James, and not just any date, a date to a family function where I was going to meet his sister. I wasn't one to overanalyze things, but call me crazy—that seemed like a pretty big deal.

Here was a man who'd told me only a couple of days ago that not only was he too busy to date but that I was too young for him, and now here I was about to attend his sister's book launch as his plus-one.

I felt hopeful, and maybe slightly delusional, that Marcus might be changing his mind about the idea of something more. And all I could suddenly hear in my head was Tate telling me, *I seem to remember a certain lawyer who didn't like to* date *either, and he's a happily married man now.*

"You're unusually quiet."

I startled, and when Marcus frowned, I chuckled. "Sorry, I was just thinking about something someone said to me the other day."

Marcus pressed the up button on the elevators. "Do I need to hurt someone?"

I couldn't have stopped my grin for all the money in the world. "First you threatened to fire Ryan for bad-mouthing me, and now you're promising acts of violence if someone was mean?"

Marcus trailed his fingers down my cheek to my chin and gripped it, then he pressed a hard kiss to my lips as the elevator *dinged* and opened behind him.

"When it comes to you, I'm beginning to think there's no rule I wouldn't bend. That includes if someone hurts you."

My breath caught at the sincerity of his words, but then

I nipped at his lower lip and laughed. "No one hurt me, I promise."

His eyes narrowed as though he were trying to decide if I was telling the truth. But before the elevator left us there on the ground floor, I quickly sidestepped him and walked inside.

"What floor is she on?"

Marcus slipped his hands into the pockets of his pants and then walked inside. As he reached around to press the number sixty-nine, I glanced over my shoulder and arched a brow.

"Really? Sixty-*nine*?"

Marcus's eyes fell to my mouth as the doors slowly shut. "I told you, she's a romance writer. She felt like it was fate."

I turned around and walked Marcus back to the wall and then couldn't help but slip my fingers under his lightweight black sweater. "Does that mean anyone that sets foot on that floor is subject to the same fate?"

"It could..." Marcus braced his hands on the rail behind him, inviting me to touch some more. I slid my palms across his warm, tight skin then moved in between his legs. When I kissed my way up the side of his neck, he groaned.

"Careful, Gabe. This elevator moves fast."

I could feel him growing hard behind his pressed pants and frowned. "That's a shame."

"I never thought so until now."

I smoothed my hands back down his tense muscles and copped a quick feel of his hard-on. "Maybe we can revisit this later?"

"Jesus, tonight suddenly got a whole lot longer," Marcus said. I took a step back, and his scorching gaze burned a trailed down to my own erection.

I quickly shoved my hands in my pockets in an effort to keep them off myself, and just as well, because the elevator stopped and the door slid open.

"We're not done with this conversation," Marcus said as we stepped out into the hall.

I glanced at him out of the corner of my eye and smirked. "No?"

"No. Now get your sexy ass down the hall before I pull you back in this elevator and hit the fire alarm."

I laughed and headed off in the direction he indicated, and when we reached the far end, I came to a stop by a door. "How many condos are on each floor here?"

"Two, I think."

That made sense. Unlike mine and Ryan's apartment building, which housed a whole lot more, these condominiums were high-end all the way. Including the square footage, apparently. Marcus's sister must be damn good at the "writing a book" thing.

Marcus raised his hand, about to knock, but before he did, I grabbed it.

"Hey?" I said, suddenly nervous about making a good impression. "Before we go in there, what's she like? Your sister?"

Marcus lowered his hand and reached for mine. "Are you nervous?"

"No."

"Are you lying?"

"Maybe."

"Well, there's no need. Abby reminds me a lot of you, actually. She's confident, creative, sweet, and full of life. The complete opposite to me in every way."

"Oh, I don't know, you're *very* confident and occasionally sweet."

When a furrow appeared between his brows, I laughed.

"I mean, not every person exacting revenge would've sent their driver to pick up their enemy at four in the morning from Starbucks."

"It wasn't four in the morning."

"It was close, and that was sweet. In a very Marcus St. James kind of way."

"I have no idea what that means."

"Of course you don't. Just know it was sweet."

He eyed me for a beat and then said, "You have nothing to worry about. Abby and I, we're very close. If I like you, she'll like you. It's as simple as that. Now, are you ready to go inside?"

I nodded, more at ease now, and when Marcus knocked, any lingering nerves disappeared because, somehow, I'd managed to convince this extraordinary man that I was worth bringing home to meet his sister. Did I really need anything more than that to boost my confidence? I glanced at Marcus's strong profile and thought hell no.

Not a second later, the door was pulled wide. In front of me, in a stylish black and gold caftan dress, was a woman around my height who was the spitting image of the man beside me. With long blond hair that cascaded in soft waves over her shoulders, Marcus's sister Abby had the same piercing blue eyes as her brother. But while his often came off cold and calculating, hers were warm and inviting as they did an inspection of me, and they seemed to sparkle when she smiled.

"Well, hello, you must be Gabriel."

Of course Marcus had introduced me that way. It was so proper, so formal, but not wanting that to be the way she felt she had to act around me, I smiled and held my hand out to her.

"That's right, but my friends call me Gabe. Marcus does too, on occasion."

She shook my hand as she looked at Marcus.

"He's right. I always call him Gabe, unless for some reason he tells me otherwise."

At the not-so-subtle jab, I looked to find Marcus aiming a pointed look my way.

"Gabe it is, then. I'm Abby, and I'm so happy to meet you. Come in, come in."

I could hear the distinct throb of music in another room, and as we stepped inside the crowded living area, the chatter of people filled the air. She leaned up to kiss her brother's cheek, and as I looked at the two side by side, I shook my head.

"Your parents must've had some pretty powerful genes. You two could be twins."

Marcus scoffed. "Twins except I'm eight years her senior."

"As if anyone can tell," she said, mirroring my exact thoughts. "I'm so pleased you're both here tonight. When Marcus said he was bringing someone, I almost didn't believe him."

Me either, I almost said, but something about giving voice to that particular doubt felt too much like tempting fate. Instead, I kept things light.

"What can I say? I'm nothing if not persistent when I want something."

"*Oh.*" Abby pointed at Marcus. "You're in trouble with this one."

Marcus eyed me for a beat, his expression growing serious, then he nodded. "Trust me, I know."

Abby reached for my hand and tugged on it. "Come with me and I'll show you around. Then I'll grab you both a copy of my book and sign it for you."

"I can hardly wait." Marcus's droll tone made Abby swat his arm as she tugged me past him. She led me through a throng of people milling around in groups, some of whom she waved to, and some of whom she actively avoided. When we slipped out onto a balcony that was so high up I figured I just might be able to meet God, I saw a mammoth table full of books, and right next to it was one that housed food.

My stomach growled—I was thankful for the music playing—as she led Marcus and me toward the piles of books all neatly stacked on top of a red tablecloth. When we reached them, she let go of me to pick one up. I looked down to see an extremely attractive man on the cover aiming a smoldering stare my way and whistled.

"Isn't he gorgeous?" Abby leaned into my side. "Look at those eyes, that jaw line—he was made for a romance cover, am I right?"

She wasn't wrong—the man was beautiful. But if we were talking strong jaw lines and magnetic eyes, she should look closer to home. If anyone had ever belonged on a romance cover it was Marcus, because damn, he'd sell millions. "I think you might be right."

Marcus took the book from me and handed it back to his sister. "And I think you should make your models wear more clothes."

A burst of laughter escaped me. Marcus aimed a cool glare my way, and I bit the side of my cheek.

"Aw, look at you getting all jealous." Abby inspected her book and nodded. "It must mean I'm right if you two are attracted to him."

"I'm not attracted to him," Marcus said.

"Okay. But you're upset that he is, so that means this guy is gold. Thank you, Gabe, for your *honest* opinion."

I laughed again as she grabbed a pen and signed a copy to each of us, and when she handed them over, Marcus took mine.

"I'll keep this somewhere safe for you."

Judging by his expression, I was thinking his fireplace

might be his definition of safe. I was about to tell him to give it back when Abby stopped one of the women passing by and asked the two of us, "Drinks?"

Marcus looked at me, and as if he knew exactly what I was thinking, he turned back to the lady and said, "We'll each have a dirty martini, thanks."

The woman nodded and then headed off to make the drinks. As I watched her go, I noticed a harried man making his way through the crowd toward us. Abby quickly slipped an arm through both mine and Marcus's and directed us back inside to the living room.

Marcus glanced over his shoulder and then back to his sister with a frown. "Is there a reason we're avoiding Mike tonight?"

"Oh, you know, the usual. He's on me about my upcoming book. What's the new premise? How many books will it be, yada yada, yada."

"Only all of that, huh?"

"Yeah..."

"And what parts of that are you missing?"

Abby turned to me, scrunched up her nose, and said, "All of it." She let out a sigh and looked back to her brother. "You can't rush these kinds of things, Marcus. It has to be spontaneous, organic. No one can create under pressure."

"I totally agree," I said.

Both of the St. James siblings turned my way.

"You write?" Abby asked as the waitress found us with a tray full of drinks. Marcus passed one of the martinis my way, and I took it and thanked him.

"Not books, no. But sometimes music."

"Music?" Abby took a sip of the champagne she'd requested. "You're a composer?"

"No. Oh God, no. I play. But occasionally I dabble in composing."

"There you go," Marcus said, gesturing to me with his glass. "You should write about a musician, a cellist. You could ask Gabe for any research you might need."

A spark of interest entered Abby's eyes as she sidled closer to me. "You play the cello?"

"I do, but I've had to take some time off to heal an injury I got last fall."

"The cello..." She tapped at her chin, and I could see the wheels turning behind her eyes.

"He's being modest," Marcus said. "He doesn't just play the cello; it's like...he becomes one with it. We went to the symphony the other night, and at the end of it he got up on stage and played 'Moon River.' It was truly one of the most magnificent things I've ever seen."

I could feel my cheeks flush under Marcus's praise. When I looked at him, the expression on his face was full of the same emotion I'd seen that night—admiration.

"Wow, you two really are meant for each other. Marcus loves anything classical music, and here you are, the mysterious young maestro."

I wasn't sure why, but for some reason I expected Marcus to immediately refute that. But when he stood there silent, I allowed the fantasy of him wanting me forever to again take flight.

"I'd love to hear you play some time," Abby said, pulling me out of my daydream.

"Uh, sure." I nodded. "We could set that up."

"I'd *love* that." She gently shoved Marcus in the arm. "You, my darling brother, just gave me a fantastic idea. Picture this: the young, beautiful musician and the beast. You know, like the grumpy guy who is always frowning but comes to life when he hears that soul-stirring sound?"

Marcus glanced at me over the rim of his glass, and the expression in his eyes told me he knew exactly who she was talking about.

Then Abby was off again. "Do you mind if I borrow Gabe for a minute?"

Marcus opened his mouth and looked like he was about to protest, but at the last second shook his head. "Of course not, as long as it's okay with Gabe."

I didn't want to go anywhere that he wasn't. But when Abby aimed excited eyes in my direction, I couldn't say no. "Okay. Sure."

She hooked an arm through mine, but just before she went to pull me away, Marcus reached for my hand and caught my fingers. "Don't be gone too long, okay?"

My heart thumped a little faster. "Promise."

"Aw, you two are so cute together."

Marcus frowned, but I couldn't tell if it was due to the word *cute* or what Abby's statement implied.

"Okay," he said, looking at his sister. "If you're going, go. But bring him back in one piece, okay?"

"I will."

The next thing I knew, Abby was leading me through the crowd away from Marcus, and all I could think was how quickly I could get free and make my way back to the grumpy guy who always frowned.

CHAPTER 35

MARCUS

IT FELT LIKE an eternity had passed since Abby stole Gabe away and whisked him off to no doubt impress her agent with the new story she had cooking. As I finished off my second martini, I found myself growing anxious to reunite with him and get him somewhere private so I could show him just how much I missed him—and wasn't that an eye-opener?

I couldn't remember the last time I'd ever missed someone's company, and the fact that it was happening now, with Gabe, was just another sign that it was time to end this, to face reality.

This illusion we were living wasn't real. I wasn't the right man for someone like him. I lived to work; that was just who I was. I was on call twenty-four seven, and someone like Gabe? He deserved more than that.

I sucked the last olive off the swizzle stick in my drink and couldn't help but think of the night we'd met. Gabe had relentlessly pursued me that night. He'd teased, tortured, and seduced me all within a couple of hours, and when I caught sight of him now across the room with Abby's agent, I felt like we were coming full circle. I wanted to touch him, feel him, and claim him as mine for one more night, and suddenly the only thing on my mind was getting him somewhere so I could do just that.

In his jeans and a loose white linen shirt, Gabe appeared relaxed and carefree. His hair was tousled, his silver chain caught on the lights every now and then, and that heartbreaker grin lit up the room whenever he decided to let it come out to play.

Several of the women gathered nearby stopped to look as Gabe laughed at something Mike said. But when Gabe's eyes finally zeroed in on me and he realized he was being watched, everyone else might as well have disappeared. It'd been the exact same way the first time our eyes locked—BOOM; the world exploded.

I was about to walk over there and make up some excuse to steal him away when a hand on my arm demanded my attention. Annoyed by the interruption, I frowned, looked at the intruder, and almost groaned. Benton Hale, one of the anchors at ENN's rival station. He was also, if rumors were to be believed, Alexander Thorne's ex.

"I thought it was you over here, but I couldn't be sure," Benton said, not bothered in the least by who I was and the fact he was encroaching on my personal time and space. "I mean, what's the likelihood that someone as lofty as Marcus

St. James would be at some run-of-the-mill romance writer's book party?"

The smarmy look on his smug face, and condescending tone toward Abby, was enough to make me want to punch him right in it. But I held myself back. I was here to support my sister, whom I loved dearly, and I would not cause a scene by drawing attention to this moron and his small-minded opinions.

I was about to brush him off and track down Gabe when Benton's fingers once again found their way to my arm.

"Now that I know it's you, however, I was hoping to catch a minute alone."

"And here I was hoping the exact opposite." If I thought my cool tone would deter him, I was out of luck. Benton ignored my irritation and forged right on ahead.

"A little birdie says that Brian Evans is looking for a new job. Does that mean a spot on *News Day* is opening up?"

It didn't, but even if it had, Benton Hale would be the last person I'd consider. He was a good enough journalist, but he was a...slimy one. He had very little integrity, was in it for the fame, not the news, and, quite frankly, I couldn't stand him.

"I haven't heard that, no. But if I were you, I wouldn't put in your letter of resignation over at ABC just yet."

"But I heard—"

"I don't care what you heard," I said, just about done with him. "I don't deal in rumors, Mr. Hale, and that is one of the key factors as to why you will never work for ENN as long as I am president of its news division. Brian

Evans is still very much a part of our company, and I find it completely disrespectful and in poor taste that you are chasing after his job. I wonder what Luis would think if he heard you were sniffing around while still under contract?"

Benton's mouth opened and shut a couple of times, and then I added, "And the next time you decide to come to a party, eat the food, and then insult the hostess, it might be smart to read up on who her brother is. That's just shoddy journalism, Benton, and my sister could write circles around you. I trust you'll see yourself out."

With that parting blow, I scanned the room in search of Gabe, but he was no longer where I'd last seen him. Frustrated, I walked through to the living room and spotted him talking with several people over where we'd first come in. As I weaved my way through the crowded room, it was as though he instantly felt me.

Gabe glanced past the woman in front of him and caught sight of my approach.

"Hello." I kissed his cheek and reached for his hand. "I was wondering if you'd like to go and get something to eat."

Gabe smiled and nodded, and after he excused himself, I tugged him toward a closed door just off to the side of the front entrance.

"Uh, I thought we were going to go and get something to eat?"

"We are." I opened the door to a small walk-in closet, pulled him inside, shut it behind him, and flicked on the light. "But I thought we'd grab your coat first."

As Gabe's back hit the door, a sinful smile curved his lips. "I didn't bring a coat."

"No?" I braced my hands by his head and leaned in to whisper against his lips, "Are you sure? I could've sworn you had one stored in here."

"Mr. St. James, I'm starting to think you have a penchant for getting up to trouble in risky places."

"I think I have a penchant for getting in trouble with *you*."

Gabe chuckled and nipped at my lower lip. "Something I'll never complain about. But don't you think your sister might wonder where we disappeared to?"

"If she does, it would only be in the context that she hopes we're doing exactly this. You saw the kind of book she writes?"

"I did. I even read an excerpt. They're very explicit."

"I wouldn't know. I've never read them."

"Really? Because you're spot-on with the whole foreplay thing, and— *Ahh* shit."

I rubbed the heel of my palm between Gabe's legs and curled my fingers around his erection. "That's good to know."

"Mhmm." Gabe nodded and bit down into his lip as though trying to keep quiet, and I smirked.

"Everything okay?"

He swallowed, his eyes locked with mine, and the flush on his cheeks was a dead giveaway that he was just as into this as I was.

"It is if you don't count the fact that there's an entire

condo full of people outside and you're rubbing my dick like we're alone."

He was right, I was doing that, but I couldn't seem to help myself, and now that I had him within touching distance, I wasn't about to stop. But if he was worried about not being able to keep quiet, I had the perfect solution.

"You worried someone might hear you?"

"Aren't you?"

"No. I just want to get my hands back on you."

"Fuck." Gabe scraped his teeth over his lower lip. "That's so insanely hot."

"And so are you." I released him and took his jaw in my hand, turning his head so I could run my tongue along his cheek. "But if you're worried you can't keep quiet, I can think of a really good way to keep your mouth occupied."

Gabe groaned, and when I let him go and took a step back, he shoved off the door and lowered his gaze to my hard-on.

"You think *you* can keep quiet?" He moved his hands to my belt and unbuckled it.

"I don't know." I felt the button and zipper on my pants release, and then Gabe slid his fingers along the elastic of my briefs. "The difference is, I don't fucking care."

And I really didn't. I wanted this moment with him, and I was greedy enough to take it, no matter the risk.

Gabe's eyes flared as he tugged my clothing down past my hips. He wrapped a firm hand around my stiff cock and then gave it a nice, long stroke.

"I have a request," he said, and I had to brace a hand on the door.

"And what's that?"

"When you're shouting down the house in the next couple minutes, let it be my name they hear. I want everyone out *there* to know who you came with tonight—in all the ways."

He signed his little request by kneeling and flicking his tongue over the head of my dick, and when I reached down and speared my fingers through his hair, Gabe waggled his brows. Jesus, it was so tempting to keep him.

"About ready to shut me up now?"

"You have no idea."

With his eyes on mine, he slowly parted his lips and guided the tip of my cock to his waiting mouth.

I took in a ragged breath. Fuck he looked good, kneeling there at my feet. So good that I couldn't wait to slip further inside his hot mouth. I twisted my fingers in his hair and could hear the music and chatter beyond the door, but when Gabe braced one hand on my thigh and grabbed my ass with the other, I didn't give a fuck.

"Damn," I muttered when he dragged his lips up along my length, and I shut my eyes for a second so I wouldn't lose it before we'd even really began.

The fingers cupping my ass dug into one of my cheeks. Gabe gave me two firm pumps and flicked his tongue over my sticky slit, and my eyes flew open.

Not shy in the least, Gabe swirled his tongue around the swollen head, then angled my shaft so he could lick along the sensitive glans underneath. He was good at this, too damn good.

I shoved my hips forward, my cock sliding in along his waiting tongue. His lips closed around me, and he swallowed me down until I was nearly hitting the back of his throat.

"Fucking hell, Gabe."

He hummed out a sound of raw, guttural pleasure, and the vibration around my shaft made a shiver race up my spine. I white-knuckled the door and gripped his hair a little tighter. My breathing was coming fast now, all the blood in my head draining south, as I pushed in and out of Gabe's mouth and reveled at the delicious warmth surrounding me. He was beautiful in his submission, not something he gave over often, as he slipped his hand between my thighs to cup my aching balls.

Damn, his hands were talented, almost as talented as his mouth. He gently squeezed and fondled the tight skin and moaned around the cock stuffed between his lips. I could feel my orgasm threatening as I watched on like a greedy voyeur, memorizing every move he made for later, when he was gone.

His jeans were molded to the hard-on inside, and his shirt gaped open to reveal all of that smooth skin. That was when I realized in the back of my lust-addled brain that I needed to be careful not to come all over him like I wanted, because he had to walk out of here, and he really didn't have a coat.

I was about to tell him just that when he slipped a finger

behind my balls to my ass and massaged the hole there. Then he pulled his lips from my cock to look up at me. With those golden eyes on mine, he leaned forward and nuzzled at the V of my groin, kissing and sucking and rooting around there as his fingers played with everything within touching distance.

It was like he couldn't get enough. Like he understood that this could be it and wanted to experience every part of me, and when his stubbled cheek grazed the side of my shaft, a harsh expletive left my tongue.

"*Gabe*," I growled, and guided his mouth back to my dick.

His grunt of pleasure was muffled by my intrusion, but his desire was evident in his needy eyes. He was watching me like he was memorizing every move as he took me all the way to the back off his throat and sucked, and all common sense vanished.

My fingers curled against the door as I gripped his hair tight, and as my body tensed and then began to tremble, Gabe shut his eyes and continued to devour me. His cheeks were hollowed out and those full lips were stretched wide, and the vision of him giving himself over to me so completely was what finally did it.

I shouted his name and came in a blinding-hot rush on his tongue, my arms and legs shaking with the power of my release.

He was the most beautiful thing I'd ever seen in my life, and for this moment, he was all mine. I reached for his chin and slowly urged him to his feet, then took his mouth in a desperate, soul-crushing kiss.

The salty taste of my release flooded my senses, and when it blended with him and wrapped itself around me, I wished for time to stand still so tomorrow wouldn't come.

"Marcus...?"

I blinked him into focus, and when I looked into his eyes, the hope I'd seen swirling there, the desire from seconds ago, had been replaced, and a new emotion now stared back at me—sadness.

He knew. Without a word from me, he knew what this moment meant for us—full circle.

I brushed a thumb across his swollen lips. "Yes?"

"Take me home."

My breath caught in my throat and my chest tightened, knowing that was the last time I'd ever hear him call my place that. But as we left Abby's, I steeled myself against what was yet to come, when the light of the morning found us and this little fantasy officially came to an end.

CHAPTER 36

GABE

THE NEXT MORNING, when I stepped out of Marcus's bedroom, I stood in the hall I'd walked down only days earlier and felt an ache in the center of my chest.

I'd known it was coming, known I was getting too attached, but no matter how hard I'd tried to keep things in perspective, my ever-hopeful heart had become one hundred percent involved with this man.

I closed my eyes and took a moment, knowing the minute I walked downstairs that the end of this—whatever *this* was—really would be that much closer. I wasn't the only one feeling that way either, judging by the empty bed I'd woken to this morning. It seemed Marcus didn't want to face this any more than I did, and had we woken to one another, that would've been exactly what we had to do—face reality.

I hiked my overnight bag up my shoulder, and as I

walked down the sweeping staircase, I reminded myself that just because I was leaving, it didn't mean this was the end.

When we'd started this whole thing, it had been nothing more than a revenge plan, a deal to pay me back for deceiving Marcus that first night. But somewhere along the way, that plan had morphed into more, and despite what Marcus was telling himself, I knew I wasn't the only one who felt that.

As I passed by his office, I fully expected to find him inside, but when I saw it was empty, I kept going to the kitchen. It was empty too, but when I dropped my bag on the floor and scanned the room, that was when I saw him.

Alone, Marcus was out on the deck where we'd had dinner the other night. He was dressed for work in a pristine suit that was tailored to his powerful frame. He had his hands clasped behind his back, and as he stood there in the morning sunlight with his hair shining like gold, I had a flashback to the very first time I'd seen him.

Stunning in his solitude, it was a stark reminder of the man Marcus was. His rigid pose told me he was all business right now; playtime was over. There'd be no sadness from him. No signs of weakness. He was no doubt itching to get back to his previously scheduled life, and it would be wise to keep that in mind, I thought.

I walked to the double doors and stepped out into the crisp morning air. Already in my suit, I was dressed and ready for work. Marcus had had it dry-cleaned and pressed so Franklin could just drop me off on his way to ENN.

It had seemed the best way, the easiest when we discussed it—now it felt anything but.

I took in a deep breath and made my way across the deck, and Marcus glanced over his shoulder. My feet faltered at the warm expression in his eyes, but then he blinked and it was gone.

"Hi." I offered up a half grin, and when Marcus turned around to face me, my heart got a little trippy. He had a light blue vest on under his navy suit today, and he was so damn handsome that he took my breath away.

"Hi yourself. I was wondering if you'd make it down on your own or if I'd have to come up and get you."

I chuckled, trying my best to keep things light. "Maybe I should've held out a little longer, then."

"Hmm," Marcus said as he took a step toward me. "Maybe you should have." He reached out to take my hand. "Are you hungry this morning? Did you want something to eat?"

I wasn't, actually—my stomach was tied up with so many emotions that eating was the last thing on my mind. "No thanks. I'm fine."

He nodded and brushed his thumb across my knuckles. Then we both spoke at the same time.

"Gabe?"

"Marcus?"

He fell silent and inclined his head for me to continue, but at the last second I lost my nerve. "Thank you for an amazing week."

"Thank you," he said, and squeezed my fingers. "I can't remember the last time I had such—"

"Fun?"

His lips crooked into a smile that made my knees weak. "Yes. It was a lot of fun."

"You should do it more often. You know, have fun. It's good for the soul. Or so I hear."

Marcus looked at me like he wanted to say something, but then pulled me forward and reached for the back of my neck. As our lips met in a kiss full of longing, my eyes fluttered shut, and I sank into all of the emotions that I'd been trying to keep at bay.

"Gabe..." he whispered against my mouth, and something about the way he said it ripped at my heart. It was painful, beautiful, and one hundred percent final, and when he gently pushed me away from him, I had to order myself to let him go.

"We should get going." Marcus trailed his fingers down my cheek. "I don't want you to be late again."

He stepped around me to walk to the door, and as he did, I closed my eyes and took in the scent of his cologne one last time.

Tell him, Gabe. Tell him what you want, before it's too late. But for some reason the words wouldn't come out of my mouth, and when he called my name, I walked over to him in silence, picked up my bag, and followed him out of the house one last time.

. . .

THE DRIVE ACROSS town was maybe the quietest one we'd ever shared. We sat in the back of the Escalade and each stared out the window closest to us. I knew I didn't have long—it took ten minutes max without traffic to get from Marcus's home to Mitchell & Madison, and of course there wasn't one damn car around this morning.

I'd been tempted to slip Franklin a twenty to give us an extended tour of Chicago, but I wasn't sure how far kidnapping Marcus would go in getting him to spend more time with me, so I was going to need to find my tongue sometime in the next few minutes.

God, I was usually so confident about things. But for some damn reason I was all up in my head this morning. I could feel my heartbeat increasing with every light we passed, and when Franklin pulled up to the curb of my work building and cut the engine, I looked across to see Marcus watching me.

He had an unreadable expression on his face. But for the first time in what felt like forever, he had an edge of coolness to him, a barrier that said keep out—and before that wall completely iced back over, I had one last thing left to say.

"I don't want this to end here. I want to see you again. I want you to see me."

There, I'd said it, and as a rush of air left me, Marcus shook his head.

"Gabe." He sighed, and I felt my stomach drop. "I'm not the kind of man you want, and I'm definitely not the man who deserves you. Trust me, you're better off this way. I'm no good at this kind of thing, being in a relationship."

"Then get good at it," I demanded, then bit down into my lip, shocked by my own outburst.

"Get good at it, huh? Just like that?"

"Yes." I nodded and could feel my heart thumping. "Practice. Practice with me."

Marcus studied me, but when he said nothing, I decided that was it. I'd done all I could—any other decision was up to him.

I curled my fingers around the handle of my bag and leaned forward to tap Franklin on the shoulder. When he looked in his rearview mirror, I smiled at him.

"See you around, Franklin."

"I hope so, Mr. Romero."

God, I hoped so too. I pushed down on the handle and climbed out, and as I stepped up onto the sidewalk, I heard my name and turned to see the window roll down.

"Yeah?"

Marcus looked me over, those blue eyes not missing an inch. "When's our first practice?"

I could hardly contain the joy that filled me at hearing those four words. When I rushed back to the car and leaned in to kiss him, Marcus chuckled.

"You really mean it?" I said as I pulled back and stared into his handsome face.

"It's either that or risk you camping outside my office until I finally give in."

"You know it."

Marcus gave a half-smile and then said, "You better get going or you're going to be late."

"But I can call you? Later?"

"Yes. Call me."

I grinned and stepped back from the Escalade, and as it slowly pulled away from the curb, it was all I could do not to jump up and fist-bump the air because, holy shit—I was now officially dating Marcus St. James.

CHAPTER 37

MARCUS

BY MIDAFTERNOON MY life had been turned on its ass. I should've known it was coming—my workweek had been going a little too smoothly, but that all changed a little over an hour ago.

Earlier this morning there'd been a massive oil spill off the Texas Gulf Coast that required round-the-clock coverage and in-depth, accurate research that was taking much longer than I would like, considering we were currently on air covering this monumental fuck-up in real time.

We needed experts from the company whose drill had failed, to report on how something of this magnitude could happen and why, yet it seemed no one was coming forward at this time to lay claim. That would change soon enough, however, with the amount of journalists now digging, and when the company's name went public, I wanted to be first in line for the scoop.

We were also in the process of tracking down a marine biologist who could discuss the impacts this was going to cause to marine life and the fishing industry up and down the coast.

This was bad—really fucking bad—and as if that wasn't enough, Summit Broadcasting had sent their private plane and expected me to be on it and up in the air tonight by five.

I had a good mind to tell them I needed to reschedule and would get there when I damn well could. But Giles had sent an email that let me know it was a now-or-never kind of opportunity, and if I didn't want it then they had someone waiting in the wings who did.

New York...

It'd always been on the top of my list of places I wanted to report from. But the right time and opportunity had never come along, so I'd built my career right here in Chicago.

That wasn't the case now, however. ENN was at the top of its game right now, and I'd made it that way. But at the same time, I'd done just about all I could do here, unlike in New York, where Summit was crying out for a facelift.

They needed someone to come in and shake things up. They needed someone who could get their ship back on course. They had the platform, they had the money—the one thing they didn't have was me, and I had to admit, the terms Giles had sent over to me were very enticing. The timing for this interview, however, couldn't be worse.

I took the elevator down to the main newsroom in search of Alexander. I needed to let him know I wouldn't be here tonight and that he and Angela would be running the show.

I pushed through the main doors, and just as I expected, the newsroom was a hive of activity. Phones were ringing, people were shouting, computer keyboards were madly tap, tap, tapping, and as I headed in the direction of Alexander's office, I spotted Ryan sitting at his desk just outside of it.

I was not usually one to stop and ask permission to enter anywhere, so I wasn't sure who was more surprised when I paused in front of Ryan's desk and he looked up.

"Hi," he said, shooting straight to his feet. "I mean, hello Marc—Mr. St. James. What can I do for you?"

Had I not been in such a rush to get things all tied up and squared away, I might've taken a minute to play with Gabe's roommate a little. Ryan was a good guy as far as I could tell, and a good friend to Gabe. As he began to fiddle with his pen and dropped it, I took pity on him.

"Hello, Ryan. Is Alexander in?"

"Uh, yeah, of course. I mean, his head is kind of spinning every which way right now, but he's definitely in there."

I pointed to the closed door. "Alone?"

"Yeah, he's alone. In fact, he called a war-room meeting for about ten minutes from now, so you're just in time."

"I can't stay, but thanks for the heads-up." I gave a clipped nod and then pushed down on the handle, but before I stepped inside, I said, "Make sure there are no interruptions."

"Yes, sir."

"Very good."

I entered Alexander's office to see him with his head

down and the phone to his ear. His usually perfect hair looked messed up from his hands worrying it, and the buttons at the neck of his shirt had been unfastened, highlighting his long day. Everyone was stressed, everyone was moving at a million miles an hour, but for this one second, I needed Alexander to stop and focus.

As the door shut behind me, he looked up, muttered, "I'll call you back," and hung up the phone. Then he tossed his pen down on his desk and leaned back in his chair. "What a clusterfuck."

"You can say that again." I took a seat as Alexander rubbed his hands over his face.

He looked tired, which wasn't surprising with everything that had happened over the last six hours. Between sourcing information, writing up copy, and approving the footage and experts his team were trying to get a hold of, preparing to go on air in the middle of a disaster and stay there for the next however many hours was exhausting—even before you set foot in the studio.

"Is everyone here?" I asked. "Do you need anyone pulled in that isn't already working?"

"No, everyone's here, but trying to get information out of Piton Oil is like trying to get blood from a stone."

"Right, but everyone knows who is responsible. There are helicopters all over the scene at this point. Sooner or later, they're going to have to talk—just make sure they're talking to you."

"We're on it," he said, and then opened his desk drawer to pull out a bottle of whiskey and a glass tumbler. When I glanced at the liquor, he shrugged. "Don't judge me. My nerves are a fucking mess."

"Not judging. I was going to ask for one myself."

Alexander chuckled and reached for a second tumbler. He poured a finger in each and then slid one over to me. I picked it up, swirled the glass, and had a sudden flash of Gabe's gorgeous eyes staring back at me.

"What could you possibly be smiling about right now?"

Not realizing I *had* been smiling, I brought the drink to my lips and downed it in one gulp. "Nothing."

Alexander narrowed his eyes and took a slow sip of his drink, then he cradled the glass between his fingers and said, "You're lying."

"No I'm not."

He scoffed. "Yes you are."

"My newsroom is in chaos, one of the biggest stories in years just broke, and I have to fly out to New York in a little under an hour. Tell me what exactly you think I have to smile about?"

Alexander sat up in his seat and eyed me a little closer. "I have no idea; that's why I asked. But now that you mention it, a funny thing happened the other day. Actually, it happened twice. I came up to see you before I went on air, and guess what?"

When I said nothing, Alexander grinned.

"You weren't there."

"So?"

"Oh, come on, Marcus. You all but live at this place. But Carmen said you rearranged your schedule this week after you had dinner with some young man in your office. She also said that you, um, might've *smiled* at her. Shocking, I know."

I frowned, not liking the idea of being the subject of office gossip. "Have you been bribing my PA again?"

"No. Carmen likes me."

"Carmen might not have a job by the end of the night."

Alexander started laughing, with good reason. He knew I wouldn't survive a day without Carmen. She was going nowhere.

"She was happy for you. Leave her alone. Hell, I'm happy for you and I don't even know what for. The question is, are *you* happy for you? You're frowning awfully hard over there."

I thought about that for a second and had to admit that I was still trying to process how I felt about everything that had happened between Gabe and me.

I'd been fully prepared to let him go this morning, but then he threw down the gauntlet in the back of the Escalade, and I hadn't been able to stop myself from picking it up. But now that I had, I needed to work out what the hell I was going to do with it.

So yes, I had no doubt that I was frowning.

"I'm fine, thank you very much. I just have a lot on my mind, that's all."

"Like flying to New York?"

"Exactly."

"So, are they sniffing around?"

If anyone knew what it was like to be courted by another

station, it was Alexander Thorne. Rated the top news anchor in the country, he had his pick of where he wanted to go, and the fact he'd picked ENN and my newsroom meant a lot to me.

"They are. Vanderhall has put together an intriguing offer but has made it abundantly clear it's only on the table for a limited time."

"That time, of course, falling right in the middle of mass chaos."

"Right. So, will you and Angela be able to handle—"

"Yes. We'll be fine. This isn't our first rodeo; you know that. Plus, it's not like you're going to be unreachable."

That was true, and I trusted Alexander. He knew what he was doing.

"Okay, then that settles it." I got to my feet and walked to the door, and Alexander followed. "Just a word to the wise: you might want to clean up a little before you hit the air tonight, Alexander. ENN has a reputation to uphold."

He laughed as he opened the door and the two of us stepped through it. "Is that your subtle way of saying I look like hell?"

"I didn't think there was anything subtle about it."

"True." Alexander grinned. "Now let me be just as frank. Leave me the hell alone and go to New York, so I can get something substantial together and not embarrass myself on air when I go live."

There was no way Alexander would ever embarrass himself—he was too smart for that—but knowing I was already running late, I gave a nod and turned to leave.

When I spotted Ryan standing by his desk with a garment bag draped over his arm, I aimed a tight smile his way and made my way toward the exit.

I had a little over forty minutes to make it to the airport and on that plane, and, well, we'd see what happened after that.

CHAPTER 38
GABE

THE SMILE I woke with had pretty much been a permanent fixture on my face since yesterday morning, when Marcus dropped me off at work. I'd carried his *when's our first practice?* with me all day, thinking about the way he looked sitting in the back of his SUV all suave and sophisticated.

I still couldn't believe it, Marcus St. James wanted to date me...*me*. The too-young university dropout who almost got fired twice within the first month of his job. Not to mention the guy Marcus had had thrown out of his office building. But wouldn't that be a good story to tell one day?

The thought made me laugh as I walked into the kitchen to make myself some breakfast. It was Friday morning, and while I'd been dreading the upcoming weekend just yesterday, now I found myself wishing the day away so I could plan something with Marcus ASAP.

I'd called yesterday, just like he said I should, and when

it went straight to voicemail, I'd had to talk myself out of thinking the worst. He was busy, that was all, and I'd been right. He texted me back around noon and told me that all hell had broken loose in the news world and he wasn't trying to get out of "practice." Then Ryan called to say he'd be pulling an all-nighter, and I was really able to breathe a sigh of relief then.

Not that I thought Marcus would lie. He was too upfront about things to do that. But when I got home last night and turned the news on to see that a major oil spill had taken place, there was no doubt left in my mind that I wasn't being blown off.

I began to brew the coffee, then grabbed a mug and some milk and sugar, and moved back to the small kitchen island, where I pulled out my phone. It had just turned seven fifteen, and I was about to send off a flirty good-morning to Marcus, in the hopes of setting up something this weekend if he was free, when the locks on the front door turned and Ryan all but fell inside the apartment.

"Uh, rough night?"

Ryan looked across the living room to me and dropped his bag just inside the door. His hair was a mess, his eyes were bloodshot, and his clothes had definitely seen better days.

"Coffee," he said, holding his hands out to me. "I need coffee."

As he trudged across the hardwood floors and slumped down onto one of the barstools, I took pity on the poor guy and slid my mug over to him. I poured in some of the steaming brew and then added some milk, just the way he liked it.

"God, I'm so tired I can't even lift this mug. Do we have a straw?"

"Aww, that's kind of pitiful."

"Yeah, well, pity me. Last night was hell. I can still hear phones ringing and people shouting even when no one's around."

I smirked at Ryan's theatrics. He loved his job and thrived on moments where the newsroom went insane. But he definitely looked a little worse for wear this morning.

"How long do you have until you're due back?"

"Xander gave us until noon, and I plan to sleep in these clothes until I have to get back there."

Oh wow, that wasn't long at all, and knowing Marcus, he probably hadn't even bothered going home. Maybe I could take him some breakfast. I looked at the clock and grimaced. I didn't have time. But maybe I could send him some.

"Well, don't let me stop you. I was just about to get showered and ready for work myself. Drink all the coffee; I'll grab one on my way into work. Maybe I'll even send one Marcus's way."

Ryan rubbed at his bleary eyes, his lack of sleep clearly leaving him confused. "Send him a coffee?"

"Yeah. I mean, I know I'm no longer indebted to him, *buuut*..." I trailed off, wondering if now was the right time to tell Ryan we were going to start dating for real.

"But what?" Ryan scoffed. "You got connections in New York?"

"New York?"

"Yeah." Ryan yawned. "He flew out there last night. It was shit timing, and he didn't seem real thrilled about leaving, but rumor has it Summit Broadcasting's been sniffing around him for a while. I mean, he wasn't about to say no to a private plane coming to get him, was he?"

Wait... Marcus was in New York? For a job interview?

"Must've been a pretty sweet deal to make him want to leave in the middle of last night's shitstorm." Ryan shook his head and finally took a sip of his coffee. "I told you, *biiig* fish."

No. Ryan must be mistaken. There was no way Marcus was in New York. We'd just been talking about getting together this weekend.

"Oh, speaking of Marcus, I forgot to ask."

I blinked at Ryan, trying to shove past the confusion swirling in my mind.

"How was your week? Sorry I wasn't home last night to celebrate your freedom."

"Uh, yeah, it was good."

"Just...good?"

I scooped up my phone and nodded. "Yeah. Hey, I need to make a call, and then I'm gonna get ready. Drag your ass to bed and get some sleep, okay?"

"Okay, but I want to hear more about your week swimming with the big fish tomorrow."

"Uh huh," I said, and waved him off. I stepped inside my

bedroom and shut the door behind me, my mind now far, far away in New York City.

Was Marcus really there right now? For a *job* interview? What did that even mean? Here I'd been dreaming up dates and future plans, and Marcus was several states over making a whole new future.

Ugh, my chest suddenly felt tight again, aching like it had yesterday on the drive into work, as I tried to make sense of why he hadn't said anything about this.

Sure, we hadn't been in each other's lives all that long, but in the short amount of time we'd spent together, I'd felt closer to him than I had anyone. I didn't know how to take this new information. I still couldn't believe it was real.

Knowing there was only one way to find out, I pulled Marcus's number up and hit call. If he *was* in New York, it'd just be turning eight thirty, so I wasn't worried about waking him.

I held my breath as it rang a couple of times, and just when I thought I would be sent to voicemail, the line connected.

"Good morning."

I closed my eyes and tried to calm the voices in my head. "Good morning."

"I was just thinking about you."

"Were you now?" I swallowed and opened my eyes, and when they landed on my cello where it stood tall and proud in the corner, I remembered the night of the symphony. I remembered the respect in Marcus's eyes, and decided right then that I deserved that respect too. I deserved more than being made a fool of.

"I was."

I pushed off the door and squared my shoulders, determined to get to the bottom of what was going on here. I had been nothing but upfront with I wanted from Marcus, and while we'd danced around the issues that he had, I stupidly thought he was willing to make an effort after yesterday's promise. How wrong was I?

"So you weren't thinking about the job that you're currently in New York to interview for today?"

When silence met me, I wondered what exactly was going through his mind. But one thing I knew for certain: it wasn't me. If I had been anywhere even remotely on his mind this morning, he would've called, he would've texted—he would've told me he'd flown to another state because he was looking at a job out there.

Instead, he responded, "How did you find out about that?"

Not *I'm sorry everything happened so fast and I didn't get a chance to tell you.* Not *I was still thinking about things and this was all last minute.* No—Marcus St. James was business first, business always, and this was a stark reminder.

"Does it matter?"

"Yes. That was my personal business and was mine to tell you."

"And were you going to? Tell me?"

Marcus sighed, and I could all but see the frown on his

forehead. "If it became a factor, then yes, I would've told you."

I gave a small, self-deprecating laugh and shook my head. His complete and utter lack of understanding of how I felt was never more apparent than in that moment. "If what became a factor? Me or the job?"

"Honestly?"

I squeezed my eyes together, already knowing I didn't want this answer. "Yes."

"Both."

Right, well, if that didn't open my eyes, nothing would. I could feel my body shaking as all of the hope from yesterday got crushed by that one word, and in its place, the temper that so rarely got the better of me reared its ugly head.

"Gabe? Listen. I can't talk about this right now—"

I opened my mouth to tell him that that was fine, I was going anyway. But before I could get the words out, I heard another voice in the background, a female voice say Marcus's name.

"Mr. Vanderhall is ready when you are."

They were calling him into the interview now? Perfect. That was just perfect. "Looks like it's your lucky day. Better go in and wow them, Mr. St. James."

"Gabe." Marcus's voice was gruff, his tone full of warning, but I was done—and I made that clear when I hung up the phone and switched the damn thing off.

I wasn't going to act like some needy, desperate guy who, after the best week of his life, fell madly in love and would just wait around for someone to decide I was worth putting in an effort for—no way.

But as I stood there staring at the blank screen of my phone, there was no helping it. The heart wanted what it wanted. It didn't care how many minutes, hours, or days I'd spent with someone, and as mine fractured and splintered over a man I barely knew, the ache from yesterday returned and threatened to swallow me whole.

But I wouldn't let it. I'd atoned for my sins when it came to me and Marcus, and while I'd first approached him full of bad intentions, that was over and done with now. We were on an even playing field as far I was concerned, and I was done chasing him. I was done begging.

Marcus St. James could do whatever the hell he wanted, and if he wanted *me*, then he could come back here and damn well fight for me.

THANK YOU

Thank you for reading BAD INTENTIONS. I hope you enjoyed watching Gabe & Marcus discover one another, because I sure had a great discovering THEM!

Make sure to join me for the next book in their journey, GOOD INTENTIONS, to see just how hard Gabe is going to make Marcus work for their HEA. ;)

You can pre-order GOOD INTENTIONS here!

Release Date: June 21st, 2021

**Love BAD INTENTIONS? Leave a review! Reviews are vital to authors, and all reviews, even just a couple of quick sentences, can help a reader decide whether to pick up our books.

If you enjoyed this book, please consider leaving a review on the site you purchased from.**

ALSO BY ELLA FRANK

The Exquisite Series
Exquisite

Entice

Edible

The Temptation Series
Try

Take

Trust

Tease

Tate

True

Confessions Series
Confessions: Robbie

Confessions: Julien

Confessions: Priest

Confessions: The Princess, The Prick & The Priest

Confessions: Henri

Confessions: Bailey

Prime Time Series

Inside Affair

Breaking News

Headlines

Sunset Cove Series

Finley

Devil's Kiss

Masters Among Monsters Series

Alasdair

Isadora

Thanos

Standalones

Blind Obsession

Veiled Innocence

Pure Seduction

PresLocke Series

Co-Authored with Brooke Blaine

Aced

Locked

Wedlocked

Fallen Angel Series

Co-Authored with Brooke Blaine

Halo

Viper

Angel

An Affair In Paris

Lust. Hate. Love.

Elite Series

Co-Authored with Brooke Blaine

Danger Zone

Need For Speed

Classified

Co-Authored with Brooke Blaine

Sex Addict

Shiver

Wrapped Up in You

All I Want for Christmas...Is My Sister's Boyfriend

Jingle Bell Rock

ABOUT THE AUTHOR

If you'd like to get to know Ella better, you can find her getting up to all kinds of shenanigans at:

The Naughty Umbrella
(Facebook Group)

TikTok

Or any of the other social media links below!

And if you would like to talk with other readers who love Ella's character's from her Chicagoverse, you can find them
HERE at
Ella Frank's Temptation Series Facebook Group.

Ella Frank is the *USA Today* Bestselling author of the Temptation series, including Try, Take, and Trust and is the co-author of the fan-favorite contemporary romance, Sex Addict. Her Exquisite series has been praised as "scorching hot!" and "enticingly sexy!"

Some of her favorite authors include Nora Roberts, Tiffany Reisz, Riley Hart, J.R. Ward, Erika Wilde, and Carly Philips.

Want to stay up to date with all things Ella? You can sign up here to join her newsletter.

Printed in Great Britain
by Amazon